Ded

My family, my boyfriend, my pets, and my friends for always being by my side and encouraging me during my writing process.

Special thanks to:

Joe Wolf – My fantastic and talented editor!

Andreea Padurean and Melisabetha on Fiverr, Max, and Billy Cottrill – Fantastic beta readers!

Dani Dock – Artist of the front and back covers.

Peter de Jong – Artist of the Aethos maps.

The McElroy Family – For the hours of entertainment and amazing inspiration

1

For more information and lore,

visit:

AnnwnRP.com

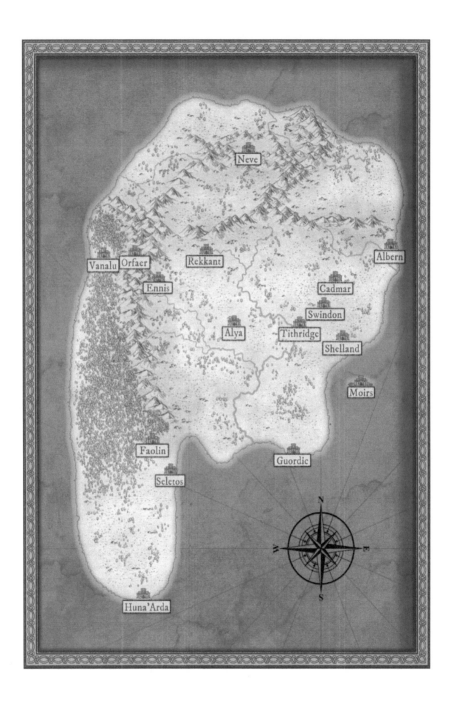

Chapter 1:

Candlelight

My awakening was in a dimly lit, damp basement, thick with the iron-tinged smell of blood. I recognized it as soon as it hit me, before even my vision could clear. But soon my vision grasped onto the sight of the person beside me. Bloody and gone was the person who lay slumped against me, their temple pressed to mine, and as soon as I saw them, I pushed the corpse away. I was startled by the bloody scene, but also by the sensation of my first emotion. It made my chest tighten, my heart quicken, and my body tremble. I didn't know at the time what this emotion was, but much later I recognized it as fear. Then, more fear as I looked around to try to get an understanding of the situation.

It was a dreary basement with a dirt floor, stone walls, and crates that lay haphazardly pushed against the walls. I sat in the center of a large circle surrounded by symbols carved into the dirt, the corpse now pushed to the side of me, and a robed young man lay on hands and knees sobbing powerfully. Richard. The name came to me, but I didn't know from where or why. I had no memory of ever having met him. This thought occurred to me as well as the thought that I didn't seem to have any memories at all. How could I have knowledge without memory? My mind swirled around this thought, gaining no real understanding from it no matter how I tried.

"Richard", I whispered to myself, holding onto the one piece of information I seemed to have.

This seemed to stir the crying teenager, and looking up, his tearful face filled with joy. Though I didn't know it yet, this was the only time I would ever see him smile. "Maria! It worked! Oh thank the gods, it worked!" he rejoiced as he pulled me into a tight hug.

The feeling of warmth was welcomed, but there was still so much I didn't know. I awkwardly pushed him away from me, hoping to get some answers. His face was warped in confusion, however, and I couldn't help but feel an emptiness growing inside of me.

"What's the matter? You don't still feel ill, do you?" His expression snapped to one of worry.

I shook my head.

"Oh good. Well what is it then?" he asked anxiously.

"Who are you? Am I? Who am I?" I began, but abruptly interrupted myself "-Oh! My voice sounds so strange." I looked down at myself the way one looks at their hands when they are lost with themselves. I found even more emotions of which I couldn't comprehend here, though. My skin was pure white, not a white that is normally flushed with the pinks and reds that live in skin, but a white that one expected to find on their sheets.

Whiter than the corpse that I had pushed away, my skin was yet another thing to pull out strange emotions from me. But I couldn't dwell on this for more than a brief few seconds before Richard shook me.

6

"What? No, that can't be! You must be joking with me, dear sister. You must be!" I looked back up to see him wearing a mask of distress, horribly terrified and confused.

I simply shook my head again, not knowing how to respond to so many words that offered me more questions than they did answers.

His face shrank and soured, with more sadness and regret playing upon it. "This can't be! I studied and adjusted everything to perfection. This isn't possible!" He broke down again and clutched at his sides as though trying to hold himself together.

I awkwardly shifted there, waiting for him to piece himself back together so I could hopefully get some answers, but after several long moments it became clear that he was incapable of doing so. I reached out a gentle hand and placed it on Richard's shoulder. Instantly he flinched away from me and snapped a hateful look in my direction. For a small second he seemed to regret this, but then he doubled down. Standing to his full height and swiping away his tears, he folded his arms as he glared at me. "I don't know where I went wrong, but you are not my Maria, that much is clear."

"R-Richard." I whispered again, still grasping at threads of sense.

He faltered for a moment, once more tears filling his eyes, but just as soon as they had arrived, he pushed them away, and instead lashed out at my face. "You will address me as Firnyn." He said while adjusting the glove on the hand he had just slapped me with. My first taste of pain left a sickly curdling in my stomach and tears in my eyes. This was the first of much pain to be had under Firnyn's care.

7

Firnyn was a strict person who demanded perfection. He treated me as an unruly dog until I managed to meet his expectations. Truthfully, it was not hard to see what he wanted from me. He wanted to forget I existed. It didn't take long for me to piece together the moments of my first memory where Firnyn spoke, and to realize that I used to be his sister. Some way or another, he had taken me from the corpse that used to be my body and put me in this one. But something had gone wrong, and I had no memory of ever having been related to him. This simply tore him apart, and I had a strange connection to what he was experiencing. So, in the beginning with just the two of us, I rapidly adapted to being seen, not heard, and never showing an ounce of the emotions that I could never place for myself. Even emotions that made me smile or laugh called for a beating under Firnyn's hand, and so I learned what I assumed to be the ways of the world. I resigned to the fact that whatever I was, I was better off forgotten.

Before I learned my lesson, no matter how I asked or pleaded or begged, Firnyn would never tell me what I was, nor who I had been. I was different from him and others like him. I was fully aged, and as seasons passed, he felt the sting of their passing, turning from a young teenager to a full-fledged man. While my skin, on the other hand, never tarnished with wrinkle nor line. I also found that I ate differently. He would eat organic matter, fruit, meat, vegetables while I was only nourished through the consumption of wax. Wax was really the strangest aspect, but the most relevant to my predicament, it seemed, as I held a stark resemblance to that of a candle. My skin was supple and smooth, but would melt if I got too close to the fireplace. And my hair at the very top of my head spiked upwards into a point where there sat a wick. A wick that was never to be lit nor cut according to Firnyn, because he deemed it "wasteful." I was this creature I had

8

no knowledge of, and I was being cared for by a man that refused to tell me what I so longed for. But after several beatings I learned to keep ahold of my search for answers and once again show no emotion.

After several years that blurred together into a shape of only nonsense and pain under Firnyn's wrath, Firnyn decided to make more of my kind. I was forbidden to see the process of making the "creatures," but he was open in the fact that he would be granting me "siblings."

The first day of my siblings' existence started violently, as Firnyn and two hooded men dragged a Satyr couple down into the basement as they kicked and screamed. I covered my ears for an hour as the screams echoed up to the living room. But then, they stopped, and shortly afterward, my siblings of metal and bone rose from the basement at Firnyn's command. They did not look like me at all, but they did seem to have the same innate need for answers that I did. I felt my heart skip with anticipation to have new people to talk to, even if only in secret.

Firnyn seemed to enjoy their presence, though he barely showed it. He even gifted my siblings a courtesy that he deemed unnecessary for me, a name. The metal being was named Reeve. His large frame made him a formidable sight, but he was gentle and quiet. It didn't take him any time to get used to Firnyn's unspoken rules of showing no emotion, and I found myself envious of how easily he navigated Firnyn's temper. My other sibling was the exact opposite of Reeve, though. Named Ultha, she was made of bone, was even slimmer than my small frame, and had a temper that rivaled even Firnyn's. She had very little patience for Firnyn's orders, and even less patience for his punishments. Despite her temper, though, she was exceedingly sweet to me.

I tried my best to spend time with both of them, catching simple sweet moments of hushed conversations and laughter as we did our daily tasks. Over the next few months, I began to grow a feeling of affection and trust toward both of them, genuinely viewing them as my siblings. But soon, despite me not even knowing the emotions I felt, Firnyn somehow noticed, and decided that his usual punishments were not enough for this slight against him. So, just three months after making my siblings, Firnyn did away with me. He assigned my siblings all the tasks I had normally been assigned, and he hid me away. He forced me into a closet where he stored his large supply of candles. I had seen the dreary closet a few times as I retrieved the candles from within to eat once a week. But now it looked a bit different. There was a small cot, a single book, and some matches.

The day I was first forced into the closet, he had dragged me from my usual place in the corner of the kitchen by the window, up the few flights of stairs to his study, and locked the door shut. I was full of emotions that made my heart ache in the beginning of those days in the dark. It hurt to think that the only light I'd ever see again was that from beneath the door or from the matches. It hurt to think of never again seeing the gentle rolling hills outside the tower. It hurt to think of never again seeing my little sitting spots for being seen and not heard. And it hurt to think of never again seeing Ultha and Reeve. But as the years in the closet passed, that emotion eventually faded into a complacent acceptance. I was locked in here, and nothing I could do would ever change that. I stayed in the closet locked away for several years. This period of time blurred together, though, so I was unsure of how much time passed and my memories of that time are a mix of silence, darkness, and treasured moments where I heard my siblings' voices.

But then, there was the day the closet opened.

Chapter 2:

And His Name Was...

My name was Luis Rockwell, renowned adventurer and slayer of all evil that plagued my beautiful home country of Aethos. Having just spent the last five years traversing the land and saving lives, I was a spritely ninety-eight years old when the United Races of Annwn (the world's leading governmental body, separate from any country, on addressing race issues) summoned me to an emergency meeting. The URA's meeting location was unknown to most people, and even as I was summoned to attend, I myself didn't know its location. On that particular Sunday afternoon, I was summoned by a portalmancer who arrived directly in my living room. I admittedly threw my teacup at him at first, but he soon cleared things up by offering me an official sealed scroll from the URA. It didn't detail much, just that my presence was urgently needed.

"Typical higher ups, not caring about interrupting the lives of the adventurers they seek to hire, ey spooky man?" I chuckled and tossed the scroll back to the hooded figure before putting on my armor and grabbing my gear pack. "Well, let's get to getting, Spookster."

The man rolled his eyes at his new nickname but began recasting his portal anyway. It took several minutes, but soon a flat, ovular disc of pure light opened before us. I stepped through into what appeared to be a small clearing in a forest. All around us, there was a large shimmering forcefield, likely to hide the area and prevent people from entering it. In the center of the clearing sat a small, white-stoned temple. I had heard of this place in rumors before: called the Unity Temple, it was the only way to enter into the lesser dimension, one that was not limitless like the five main dimensions, that housed the actual council building. But as I looked it up and down, I couldn't help but chuckle as it was much more diminutive than the rumors made it out to be. Not much more than a one room hut, it was difficult to see how it garnered the name of "temple," and I chuckled to myself.

Spookster paid no mind to me, and immediately walked through the arched opening. I followed quickly behind him, and as my eyes adjusted to the darkness, they were all at once blinded by a bright white light. I rubbed my eyes and eventually, I saw its source. Spookster had activated something in the temple to cause a bright white rectangular plane to form in the temple's center. I shrugged and immediately stepped forward, ready to go into the portal, but was stopped when Spookster stepped out in front of me.

"I have been told to advise you before your entrance that your manners and silence in front of the representatives are of the utmost importance. You do not speak unless spoken to, you do not yawn, or cough, or sneeze, and most importantly, you stand and bow when the representatives enter the room. Is that clear?" His voice was as slimy as he seemed, and almost made me shudder in disgust.

I didn't like manners or the requirement of them, but I nodded nonetheless, knowing that I would not want the URA of all things to be on my bad side.

"I've got it covered, Spookster. Don't you worry your creepy little head about it." I smiled wide and patted him on the shoulder before gently pushing him aside and stepping through the portal.

On the other side, it was clear that we had entered a lesser dimension as the sky was purple and had no sun, but instead had tiny floating orbs of magic to light the whole place up. I whistled in amazement, stopping in my tracks as I looked at it all. Immediately in front of me, there was a white stone path that led through the glimmering waters, to the only building in sight. The URA building was excessively grand and made entirely of pristine white marble. It was easily one of the biggest buildings I had ever seen, and I couldn't help but gawk at it as I stood there. I was quickly shaken out of it by a derisive snort from Spookster that made me snap my head back towards him. He flinched, but then I smiled wide, and he relaxed a bit.

Spookster led me forward along the path and into the building through a large set of iron-clad double doors. These seemed out of place to me; a solid metal barricade in a place so formal and calm. Inside, there was a large entrance hall, complete with several large staircases, a fountain, and more floating orbs. More glaringly obvious, though, were the flocks of hooded figures that swarmed about the place.

"Well, I'll be damned, there's a whole colony of Spooksters! Good to know you aren't a loner, buddy," I joked, patting him on the back.

He glared silently at me, and I cleared my throat awkwardly, motioning with a hand for him to continue walking. He sighed but obliged, guiding me further into the grand building. We then ascended staircase after staircase, until finally we reached the top floor and the council's meeting hall. With exactly fifty race and subrace representatives elected to the URA, the hall was fitted with a huge circular table that could easily accommodate eighty people, or so I guessed. We were apparently the first ones there, as the room was empty. Spookster continued to guide me over to the lefthand side of the table where there sat a small cabinet. He reached inside the cabinet and pulled out a small gem on a necklace which he handed to me.

"Aw, for me? Spookster you shouldn't have! Now all the other girls will be jealous!" I said in a high-pitched voice, barely keeping a straight face.

He simply glared at me silently once more before he finally spoke up again. "Just put on the crystal. It's been enchanted to project your voice throughout the room. But remember, no speaking unless spoken to!"

"Don't worry so much, Spookster! I'll be the vision of respect." I said as I clipped the necklace around my neck, careful not to get it caught on my scales. I bopped him gently on the nose with a finger and moved to go sit at the table.

Spookster recoiled, but with an aggravated sigh, he called out to me. "It's the chair labeled with your name!"

I moved around the table and found that the chairs were positioned in alphabetical order according to Common, the official world language as decided upon by the URA. I easily found my chair and promptly plopped down into it, folding my hands in front of me. I only had to wait a few minutes before the representatives began filing in. One by one, guided by their own hooded figures, one person of each of the fifty races and subraces entered the room and sat at their assigned seats. Most of them didn't pay me any mind, but the Wynorm representative, a dragon-like humanoid of my own race, made sure to bow his head to me in respect. I quickly followed suit. I straightened up a little too fast though and felt

14

blood rush to my head. I tried to hide my wooziness and sat my head on my hand, propped up on the table. I was snapped back to reality as the head council member of the URA entered the room. A beautiful Karchi woman, a large cat centaur, strode gracefully into the room, her many golden adornments clinking gently as she walked. She exuded authority, though in reality she held no more power than any of the other representatives. She was merely appointed to call and guide meetings. I was easily taken in by her beauty and grace, but soon steeled myself as I knew the meeting was about to start.

"Welcome," she began with a heavy accent, bowing her head in the council's general direction. "It is time, in the year of Lakshmi 706[1], to convene here once again to address a terrible act that affects all races and must be addressed. I know that many of you are weary as the most recent council meeting was only six years ago, but I ask for your patience and understanding that this matter is extremely important and could change the world for the worse if handled incorrectly." She paused for a moment to look around the room, and then gestured to one of the hooded figures that lined the walls. They quickly ran up to her and bowed, presenting a scroll from which she began to read. "In the year Lakshmi 680, a heinous act was committed by a wizard known to many as Firnyn. He has accomplished what we previously thought impossible and has twisted it to his own perversion. What I am about to show you may shock and disturb you, but I ask that you look on, for the sake of common decency." She then motioned again towards the hooded figures.

---

[1] The God Year system created by the URA, a God Year is a period of 1,000 years marked alphabetically by the name of a God/Goddess. So Bromios 757 would be the year 2757 and Jupiter 003 would be the year 10,003. Lakshmi 706 is the year 12,706.

This time, three hooded figures moved forward, one with a mask covering their face as well. The masked figure stood closest to the woman, and slowly took off their hood and mask to the gesture of the woman. The being before us was a humanoid golem made of leather, and whispers instantly began to spread as everyone was confused. A golem was not unheard of, and some creators liked to make their golems look humanoid. But then, everyone's voices caught in their throats in surprise and horror as the golem began to speak.

"Hello. I have not been given a name to tell you, but I have come before you today to prove my and my siblings' existence and ask for your help. I did not choose to be created, and I know in my soul that we were forced into this existence. And I and you know this to be a crime against all things good in our world of Annwn. So please, consider my request with your hearts, not the disgust that comes with my existence." The golem bowed their head low and waited as the representatives reacted.

The entire room was in an uproar, and I watched in numb shock at it all. This couldn't be happening, could it? There were the laws of nature, and this was clearly a perversion of all of them. Golems were strictly made of inferior souls, souls incapable of abstract thought and known for little spiritual progress over lifetimes. But this? This was impossible. Yet the impossible stood before us, bowing its head. Somehow, this Firnyn guy had created golems with superior souls, souls that normally only humanoids and dragons can possess. Now there were Elementals created with superior souls, but there were built-in rules, one of which was the soul had to be willing. But this wasn't a willing soul, and clearly wasn't an elemental since it was made of leather and Elementals could only be made of air, fire, water, or earth. This had to be a use of dark magic, and I knew it when I saw it, for my people had an

16

affinity for this magic that most pretended didn't exist. My mind swirled with the possibilities of what this could do to the world. If this magic was free, it could be used for widespread torture, curses, and even to build entire armies.

"This is twisted! There is no reality in which we should allow them to exist! *That* would be how to help them best." The Angel representative spoke up, and several representatives made sounds of agreement.

"Nonsense! As the little one says, they did not choose this. To kill them without their consent would be further tragedy!" said the sign language interpreter for the Giant representative, as Giants were all born deaf. This sentiment was echoed by many more representatives, and it seemed it was the majority vote.

Just to be sure, though, the council leader called out to quiet everyone down, and announced a vote. "All representatives that view these golems should be killed, please raise your hand." The Angel and six other representatives raised their hands. "All representatives that are against the killing of these golems, please raise your hand." Everyone else at the table, other than me and the interpreter, raised their hands. "Then it is settled, they should be held to the same right to life as any one of us. Now, tell us please, how many of you are there?" she asked.

"When I escaped, there were four of us including myself, but on the night I escaped, I overheard Firnyn's goons talking about the wizards in the Wastelands that had begun to use the spell themselves. I am unsure how many exist there." They said, still bowing their head low.

More chaos erupted, and more arguing commenced. After an hour of bickering, they came to a conclusion: Firnyn should be killed, and his research destroyed. As for the wizards in the

Wastelands, nothing could be done except hope that the spell stayed within the continent. The Wastelands were a treacherous place, full of dark energy radiated by the crystal Malkeshin, which appeared during Bromios 001, and caused the continent once full of life to be laid to waste. Plants died, evil aligned creatures flocked to it, and a thick fog that burns the lungs filled the air. The crystal's effects were widespread at first, causing magical plants and animals to rampage, destroying crops, villages, and cities alike. But thanks to some of the world's most powerful mages, the energy of the crystal was confined to the continent that housed it, thus creating the Wastelands.

"Now that we have reached a plan of action, I'd like to direct your attention to our guest. Please introduce yourself, Luis." The council leader said, extending a hand towards me.

I shot up, the chair squeaking hard against the polished floor, and awkwardly straightened myself, raising my head high. "My name is Luis Rockwell: renowned adventurer and slayer of all evil that plagues my beautiful home country of Aethos!" I announced probably a little too loudly as the crystal necklace made my voice boom in the room.

"Really? A Wynorm? Is that the best idea? They do tend to dabble in the darker magics…" The High Elf representative sneered as he looked me up and down.

I opened my mouth to throw a quip back at him, but was interrupted by the Satyr representative. "You seem to forget yourselves if you think that race is the only factor in determining someone's suitability for this task."

"I agree, while this is a matter of the races, a threat to all, we should not judge this adventurer based solely on his race." The

18

council leader silenced any dissent on the matter, but a new question quickly arose.

"You are completely correct, head chair, but another factor is more pressing. Why, pray tell, is he from Aethos?" said the Ekek, a human with a bird's head and wings.

"Precisely what I was thinking. Surely my country can offer better adventurers," the Hegal, winged demon, representative spoke up.

The room was then filled with a cacophony of yelling as each representative argued for their home country. This too took quite a while, and normally in these circumstances I may have dozed off, but this was a matter of world-wide importance. I'd be able to help the whole world if I did this quest correctly, and that had always been a dream of mine. Eventually, around the one hour mark, I stood from my chair once more. I could feel Spookster's eyes on me from behind, dreading what I was about to do. But I knew that this was going nowhere, and that I had to do something to prove my worth.

I cleared my throat loudly, but no one paid me any attention at all, so I promptly climbed up onto the table and stood there instead. This caught everyone's attention, and I could feel anger from several of the representatives, but I continued, nonetheless. "My name is Luis Rockwell, as I stated before, and I'm sure that many of you have no idea who I am. So let me enlighten you." I began to tell the story of my greatest adventure, one where I dove into a cave swarming with evil magical beasts that had been terrorizing a local town. Beast after beast, I cut them down until I reached the main den where a monstrous creature lay in wait. "It slithered towards me like a snake, but it had no scales and far too many muscular legs. Its face was hideous, a face only a mother could love-kind of face." This drew a few chuckles from some of them. "But indeed it had a face like that of a Human man and a mane of spiked black fur surrounding it. Truly a thing of nightmares was this baby. But I didn't hesitate! I flew forward, careful to dodge the swarms of smaller creatures that clung around it like a child to its mother, and brought my sword down upon its thick writhing neck. It tried to retaliate in its last moments, as my arm began to slowly turn to stone!" Gasps echoed through the room. I had them hook, line, and sinker. I wanted to smile boastfully, but I kept my cool and continued my tale. "So, I carved out this thing's eyeballs with one hand, thinking I'd need them for an antidote, and slowly, painfully fought my way back out of the cave. I crawled out of there just as the sun had risen, and just when I thought all of me had turned to stone as well, the sunlight hit my body. In that instant, the stone faded from me, and so returned my beautiful blue scales!"

The room was filled with resounding approval, and before long the representatives voted for me to be the one to take down Firnyn.

Chapter 3:

A Battle Well Fought

The meeting finished, I had climbed down from the table and been swarmed with people, both representatives and the hooded figures, everyone wanting to talk to me or shake my hand. I did this for a least a dozen or so people when Spookster snatched me out of the crowd, pulling me along by the tip of one of my wings.

"Ow, ow, ow!" I protested, but Spookster didn't seem to care and continued to drag me around the table until he stopped in front of the council leader. I froze in place, a stupid grin on my face as I waited for her to speak.

"Luis, thank you for agreeing to come and help us with this matter. We are forever grateful." She bowed her head, and I quickly followed suit, not wanting to be seen as impolite. She lifted her head and offered me her hand. I looked between her, it, and Spookster in a panic, not knowing what she wanted me to do with it. Seeing my distress she chuckled and said, "Take my hand, and walk with me, dear Luis. For we have much to discuss."

I took her hand gently in my own and was guided out of the council room and down the many sets of stairs. Once we arrived at the entrance hall, we went straight past the stairs through an archway that led to a beautiful garden. There was another fountain here, though this one was much grander than the one in the entrance hall, and depicted a hooded figure holding a large set of scales from which the fountain's water poured out. On the thick lip of the fountain's edge is where the council leader chose to sit, her long lion frame easily jumping onto the ledge and relaxing with a heavy sigh. She patted the space on the edge next to her and I quickly sat down.

We sat in silence for more than a few minutes until finally, she spoke. "I understand that with all quests, adventurers expect and are due rewards. And the same can be said of this mission. By its end, should you find yourself successful, you will be due a reward. But the council, despite its grand appearance is quite limited in funds. The council members generally provide resources from their own coffers, unless a generous donation is made, but those happen so rarely. What I am trying to say is that we may not be able to offer you much in terms of a reward, but I ask that this not stop you from helping your country's and world's people. I ask this most humbly of you, please." She then bowed her head low, much lower than any figure of her importance and pride bows.

I swallowed hard and spoke softly, "I uh, I'm gonna be honest with you, ma'am. I didn't realize that the URA gave rewards for quests. It just genuinely didn't occur to me. But yeah, of course I'll still take the quest, I'm an adventurer after all!" I smiled wide and found that she had taken my hands in hers.

"You will not regret this, I swear it," she emphasized each word carefully as though she were trying to pin down each fluttering one to a board.

From there, she addressed the details of the quest, namely Firnyn's location and known powers. I listened intently, sure to carve each detail into my mind. As we finished our conversation, Spookster arrived carrying my adventuring pack in both hands.

"You forgot this at your chair," he grumbled as he struggled with the weight of the bag.

"Spookster! You brought that all this way, for me? My goodness, my heart will never be still again!" I gestured wildly as I easily lifted the bag out of his hands and onto my back, careful to clip it around my wings.

The council leader chuckled, "Spookster, eh? Funny, though I'm not sure he appreciates it too much." She turned to Spookster and smiled. "Eprnias, please escort Luis to the armory. And Luis, please help yourself to our selection of weapons, and get to know your assigned helpers who will be accompanying you."

I nodded and stood up, grabbing 'Eprnias' by the shoulder. "Onward, Spookster! We have a wizard to defeat!" I marched forward, dragging Spookster right along with me. I made it out into the entrance hall before I stopped, looking around. "Alright, your turn Spookster, lead the way!"

Spookster sighed heavily, but began walking, nonetheless. This time we only had to go up one flight of stairs and down a long hallway to get to our destination. The armory was certainly not the biggest I had ever seen, but it was more than enough; better than mine at home at least. Inside waited three cloaked figures, their cloaks matching Spookster's and all the others' I had seen since arriving here. Upon entering the room, the three of them bowed low and introduced themselves as 'council servants.'

"Ok, that's great and all, but I need to be able to tell you apart. I can't call you all Spookster, now, can I?" I chuckled to myself, and they looked at me in confusion.

After some more egging them on, they relented and introduced themselves as Anya (a Satyr), Hyancinthus (a Harpy),

23

and Ophelia (a Moon Elf). "Great! So, I'm calling you Hyan because there's no way I'm saying your full name every single time. Cool? Cool."

He nodded, smiling, and I knew that we would get along just fine.

I grabbed the first short sword I saw, a light and pristine sword that had an edge so sharp it might cut through reality itself. A good sword, but not as good as mine. Still, it was nice to have a backup. I also grabbed two daggers and then stood back to watch the others pick their equipment. Anya grabbed a large axe that had a red ribbon wrapped around its hilt, Ophelia grabbed a shortbow and arrows, and Hyan simply donned some leather armor. I nodded, satisfied with their choices as they all looked back at me confidently. After we raided the armory, Spookster started casting a portal spell, one that would go to right outside Firnyn's tower in Aethos. After a few minutes, the portal was ready to go, and we stepped through it and into an open field.

I breathed in deep and sighed. "It's good to be home." Even if I didn't know where in Aethos we were, Aethos was Aethos, and that meant home for me. I looked around and spotted the tower, a good two hundred feet away and standing tall against the bright blue sky. "Alright, let's do this." I cracked my knuckles and immediately started going over the plan. Hyan would fly over and land on the roof, waiting for our signal, while the three of us snuck up to the tower's door. Ophelia would pick the lock, and then Anya and I would slip inside, unnoticed. Once inside we'd find and corner Firnyn, then give Hyan the signal so he would crash into the window on the top floor. Then we'd attack! Anya swinging her axe, me swinging my sword, Ophelia supporting with her shortbow, and Hyan acting as the blockade to keep Firnyn

from escaping. Then, after a brutal battle, we'd kill Firnyn. M

success! Or at least I hoped.

We were satisfied with our plan, and immediately beg
heading towards to tower. With Hyan safely on the roof, we l
to sneak towards the door, moving as quickly as we could wit
our armor jangling. We made it to the door with no sign that
anyone saw us. But then Ophelia opened the lock, and slippe
catching herself on the door which proceeded to swing wide
and clatter against the stone of the tower wall. Standing inside
holding a cup of tea and wearing a nightgown, was Firnyn. Op
scrambled up to her feet, fumbling with her shortbow to try t
a shot at him. Anya slipped past and ran forward, axe in hand,
ready to strike. Firnyn's teacup fell to the ground, shattering a
turned to run up the stairs. He was surprisingly fast and skitte
into one of the second floor rooms. I carefully pushed past O
apologizing as my wing hit her on the back of the head, and ru
after Anya who had already begun to follow him up the stairs.
made it to the floor he had run onto, but we couldn't tell whic
the four rooms he hid in.

At the first door, Anya kicked it down, not bothering t
if it was unlocked, and a high-pitched scream rang out. Inside,
sat a pale woman who at second glance, looked to be made of

"You're one of the golems, right?" I asked as Anya hea
a sigh and exited the room, immediately heading to the next dc

She nodded, scared.

"One of you came to us, to save you guys. We're here t
help, I promise," I reassured her.

In the hallway, Anya stood before another door, ready to kick it down.

"Woah, wait. Maybe we should just carefully look inside so we don't scare any more innocent golem people?"

Anya nodded reluctantly, and I opened the door slowly, peering in. Inside there was a large golem made of shards of metal looking out the window with his back to the door. I decided it best not to disturb the hulking metal beast and slowly, silently closed the door. I moved over to the third door and did the same. Inside was a much more reasonably sized golem that appeared to be made of paper. He looked up at me expectantly when I opened the door, and beamed with happiness as he saw me. He shot up from his chair and rushed towards the door, ready to say something. I quickly put a finger to my lips and hushed him. He stopped and nodded, though he looked a bit distraught. I made a mental note to try to cheer him up after this Firnyn guy was dead. I closed that door as well, as silently as I could, then turned to face the fourth and final door. I motioned to Anya to have at it, and she instantly obliged, kicking the door in with her powerful hoof.

In that same instant, we were surrounded by a thick, purple smoke. I held my breath, hoping I hadn't already breathed any in. I peered through the smoke, looking for any sign of Anya or Ophelia, and as I stepped forward my stomach dropped, realizing that I had run into something…someone. My mind raced in those few seconds as I tried desperately to think of what to do. But then an idea occurred to me. I stretched my wings as much as I could in this small space and began beating them up and down, trying to get the cloud to disperse. The cloud blew away, and I felt a moment of pride for my quick thinking. That is until, from within the bits of smoke that clung to the room in which Firnyn had hidden, an orange lightning bolt shot out, striking into the left side of my

26

breastplate and knocking me back a step. It left a black mark with a red-hot orange center that slowly grew outwards as it burned through the metal.

Seeing this, I clicked my tongue and finally unsheathed my sword, a hefty handle wrapped in purple leather cord and attached to the beautiful steel blade that was marked at the very tip with runes. I moved through the remaining smoke confidently, sword clutched in both hands as I held it vertically in front of me. One, two, three steps forward and another bolt flew out, but this time my sword caught it and instantly sent sparks flying as it dispersed the spell with ease. Not just any old magic trick, my sword was enchanted by a skilled magic items craftsman that I had met on my journeys. Smiling, I stepped over Anya, taking note that she was in fact still breathing, and walked into the room and out of the smoke. As soon as I saw Firnyn, who now wore a red and gold robe decorated with many runes and held a gnarled wooden staff adorned with several red crystals, he cast his lightning at me again. I turned my sword horizontal and caught the bolt once more, dispersing it. Firnyn's face was a mix of rage and horror, and I could tell he didn't know whether to run or fight. I didn't give him time to think, though, and swung my sword at him, aiming for his neck. He recoiled backwards, holding his staff in front of him as he saw the attack coming, and my sword caught in the mangled mess of branches as it broke several of the crystals.

I let out a low growl in frustration, and Firnyn faltered as he began begging for his life.

Not giving him the chance to get my pity and cast a spell during my hesitation, I pulled back my sword and in one swift motion, freed Firnyn's head from his shoulders. Blood splattered everywhere, but I was used to a little gore by that point. The thing that irked me though was that it ended up being an easy fight.

27

Hearing about a great wizard that had achieved the impossible, made me think that I would have a good fight ahead of me. But this? It was lackluster, hardly a battle well fought. I gave Firnyn's head a small kick without thinking and it rolled to the other side of the room. Then, I turned to go check on Anya, Ophelia, and Hyan. Anya and Ophelia lay collapsed, Anya in the doorway and Ophelia on the stairs. Hyan came crashing down the stairs, ready to fight, only to realize that the fight had already been won. I sighed in disappointment at the whole situation, and motioned for Hyan to help me set the girls up against the wall.

After getting them situated, I went back into the rooms with the golems, and one by one told them they were now free. The bone golem seemed overjoyed, the paper golem was a bit fearful but still happy, and the metal golem showed no emotion at all. I walked the three of them out to where Spookster waited in the field, as I figured the URA would want to talk with them. Spookster seemed almost proud that I had thought of it on my own. I smiled sarcastically as he praised me, and turned back towards the tower; it was time to give this place a full sweep. I started on the first floor, nothing much there except a dining room, kitchen, and living room. The second floor was already clear. The third floor seemed to be a floor dedicated entirely to storage, and I made a mental note to dig through some of those crates later. Finally, the fourth floor was a large study, full to the brim with books and scrolls.

I looked over a few of them and grabbed a few enchanted bits for later, but then I heard something move. I spun around, looking all over the room, but there was no one here. I walked around confused until I saw a small broom closet tucked away in one corner of the room and almost completely hidden by two bookshelves positioned in front of it. I heard the sound again, like someone bumping into something, and it was definitely coming

28

from that closet. *Could it be a cat? Who keeps a cat locked in a closet?* I thought as I heaved one of the bookshelves to the side. *Shit, maybe it's some evil magical creature that he kept locked away up here!* Erring on the side of caution, I drew my sword once more after I had moved the second bookcase.

I took a breath, then flung the door open. Inside, quivering on the other side of the closet was a girl, maybe sixteen or seventeen in Human years. I instantly dropped my sword and kneeled down to offer her my hand. The light, no longer blocked by me, poured in on her, and I got a much better look at her. She was a golem made of candle wax, complete with a candle wick sitting on top of her head. This isn't what concerned me though, as she wore a ragged dress and shivered like it was ten below. She hadn't taken my hand but looked from it to me hesitantly. I smiled, took my hand, and gently placed it on her cheek. This was apparently the right move as she instantly stopped shaking and placed both of her hands on mine.

She spoke up softly, "Is he finally letting me out? D-Do I get to come outside again?" Her voice was gentle and timid, like a child's, though it was clear she was older than that.

I smiled wider. "Even better, kid. Firnyn is dead. You're free now."

Chapter 4:

What It Means to be Free

I felt the tears begin to stream down my cheeks. I dropped my hands from the Wynorm man and held myself tightly. I didn't know what I felt, nor could I tell if it was good or bad, but my entire body ached with it. The man responded with compassion and wrapped me in a tight hug. This made me recoil slightly, but when I realized he wasn't going to hurt me, I relaxed in his grasp, crying thick, heavy tears. I cried for several minutes before I was able to calm myself, and I breathed a heavy sigh as I pushed the man away from me.

"Uhm, t-thank you? I'm unsure how to say what I'm feeling, but I know that I want to thank you." I whispered.

So used to Firnyn's heavy hand, I expected retaliation, and I flinched as I waited for him to do just that. Instead, I heard him chuckle.

"Don't worry about it, kid. This is one of the easier parts of the job."

"Job?" I asked, my mind swirling with the whole situation.

"Yeah, I'm an adventurer. Here to save the day!" He smiled wide, showing his mostly sharp, pointed teeth.

This made me feel strange, an old feeling from when I first felt feeling at all. But at the same time, I also felt a gentle warmth in

my chest, and I found myself smiling back at him. He nodded, taking my smile as proof that I was ok, before moving out of the closet and into the study. It was blindingly bright, a light I hadn't seen fully in several long years, but it was beautiful. I felt myself wanting to cry again, but then I noticed the man's outstretched hand, waiting to help me out of the closet. I took it shakily, and he effortlessly pulled me up and out into the light. He held me close to him for a second, making sure I wasn't going to fall. Once he realized that I was steady on my feet, he released me. I felt a moment of loss, of a desire for that warmth, but I held my tongue and pushed the feelings down, down, down. Feelings would be punished, after all, right? I was unsure if this man would be like Firnyn, if everyone would be like Firnyn. So, I decided it safer to simply do what I had always done, and ignore it.

"Let's get to getting, kid. I've got some crates to dig through, and you have to speak to the URA," he said and turned away from me, moving towards the door.

Without thinking, I reached out a hand and grabbed onto one of his leather pouches that hung from around his waist. Realizing what I had done, I instantly dropped my hand as my mind swirled with what to do. The man turned around, confused at first, then worried as he saw my expression. Instinctively I turned away from him, and moved towards the closet; what was my prison had also become my safe place. The man grabbed my arm gently and pulled me back towards him.

"Woah, woah, where are you going? Weren't you literally just trapped in there? And I saved you? Is any of this clicking for you?" he asked, confused but also smiling.

I nodded slowly, not looking him in the eye. I didn't understand my emotions or actions, so how in the world could I

explain them to him? I fell deep into the void in my mind, spiraling down, down, down.

"Kid? You ok? You know you're safe now, right? You don't have to go back in that closet ever again," he reassured me, still gently holding my arm.

In that moment I saw a light, burning bright and beautiful against the darkness of my mind. He was right, I was safe now. Safe with him. I hung my head as my heart pounded against my chest and my cheeks grew warm. I wanted to stay by his side, and so I did. Even as he dug through the crates of the tower, as he explored the dark horror of the basement, and as he talked with several robed figures. I refused to leave his side. But then, we walked out of the tower. This was my first time ever stepping foot outside of it, and I hesitated for a moment, looking to him as my body told me not to leave. He smiled with a bit of pity in his expression, and gently grabbed my hand, leading me onwards. I took a few heavy breaths and stepped out onto the grass, my bare feet caressed by its blades. My heart wanted to leap out of my chest, to run and roll around on the beautiful hillside, but I knew better than to show that much emotion. So, instead, I simply smiled and followed along with the man. We walked past many robed figures that swarmed out of a portal nearby and then to my surprise, we headed straight through.

On the other side of the portal, I found myself in a forest of some sort with a small stone structure on one end of this clearing. We followed where the stream of robed figures came from, and stepped through yet another portal. This time, I walked into a wonderland of purple skies and tiny floating balls of light. I looked around in awe at first, but caught myself just as the man turned to look at me.

"Listen, kid. From here you'll have to go speak to the URA, but I'll be here when you finish, and then we'll likely have to attend a meeting." He smiled gently and then placed a hand on my shoulder before releasing me into the care of one of the robed people.

A hollow feeling filled my chest as the robed figures ushered me into the large marble building. It was a beautiful sight to behold inside the building, but all I could think of was getting back to the man, getting back to guaranteed safety. I followed the robes, my mind elsewhere, until we reached a small lounge area where there sat all of my siblings. Though I only knew of Ultha and Reeve, the other two were clearly made like me. As I entered, Ultha stood and immediately offered me a hug which I took awkwardly. Reeve on the other hand, stood silently behind Ultha, and when we had finished our hug, he patted my back gently and guided me over to a spot on the couch next to them.

I opened my mouth to ask about my other two siblings, wanting to know their names, but more hooded figures glided into the room. One of them spoke up, telling us that we would be examined both magically and medically to see if there was a way to help us. Ultha scoffed at this, but didn't stop them from proceeding with the examination. First came the medical exam, where they poked and prodded us with a variety of medical equipment, testing our reflexes, heartrates, organ size and placement, and more that I didn't understand. Then came the magical tests. I barely understood what they were testing for, but I heard them make surprised noises every now and then. The whole process took about an hour, and when they were finished, they left us alone in the room with the promise that they would return momentarily to retrieve us.

In the silence of the room, we all shifted awkwardly, unsure of what to say or how to say it. I took the first step, steeling myself as I slowly began to speak, "Y-You're our siblings, right? I don't recognize you, when were you made?"

The leather one spoke first with confidence, "Four months ago. I don't recognize you either, though. Who are you? Were you made by someone else?" They practically physically stepped on the paper one as they interrogated me.

I shook my head. "No, I was made by Firnyn many years ago. I was with him as his servant for about sixteen years before I...before I 'left'."

"Then where did you go?" the leather one asked with a mix of disbelief and disgust.

I hesitated for a moment, looking down at my hands, somehow ashamed of my previous predicament. "He locked me in a closet upstairs," I responded, my voice barely reaching them.

Stunned silence filled the room, and I pinched my hands together tightly as the urge to run filled my being. But then Ultha placed a gentle hand on my shoulder, trying to reassure me, and my chest filled with warmth. I looked over to her and smiled weakly, and as I did, the paper one finally spoke up.

"Two years ago...For when I was made, I mean; it was two years ago," the paper one said, somehow even more timid than me.

I went to say something else, but just then the robed figures returned to the room. They quickly shooed us out and guided us up several staircases until we entered a room with a very large circular table where there sat members of seemingly every race and subrace. I looked around frantically, searching each face for the blue-scaled Wynorm man from earlier. There was one Wynorm here, but he

had black scales. My heart felt like it dropped into my stomach as the thought occurred to me that he may have lied, and dumped me on the robed figures to get away from me. *Perhaps I was too clingy? Too annoying?* My mind raced around these thoughts until I heard someone clear their throat behind me. I spun around only to find the blue-scaled Wynorm man standing there. Every ounce of my being wanted to hug him, to thank him for not leaving me behind, but I figured that now was not the time nor the place for it. Instead, I simply smiled, to which he smiled back and then motioned for me to look back at the table of people.

A beautiful Karchi woman stood from her bench and addressed everyone. "Please let us welcome our guests warmly as we figure out exactly how to handle this situation." She turned to us and bowed her head slightly. Everyone in the room copied her and bowed towards us, to which we quickly bowed in return. "Good," she continued. "Now, we have talked in great detail about you in preparation for this moment, but we thought it only right for you to have the final say. You see, we are concerned. It is clear that the magic Firnyn used to create you was evil, but we are unsure if that magic has tainted your souls. You do not seem like it, certainly not. But as an extra precaution, you golems will-"

"Uh uh, no. We aren't golems, we're people," said Ultha as she cut off the woman.

Several people in the room gasped, and I assumed that Ultha had stepped on some toes by cutting her off. Ultha didn't seem to care though, and stared at the woman with confidence.

The woman seemed a bit frazzled by this, but extended a hand towards us. "Right, y-yes of course. What would you like to be called instead? It is your race, afterall."

"Good. I'm glad that you recognize that," Ultha said without missing a beat. Then she paused for a moment, a hand on her chin as she thought. "What about…Anathema? Since our origins aren't exactly favorable, and I'm guessing people are going to treat us as such." Ultha chose a word from the Satyr language that meant 'accursed thing.' A strange choice that confused several people in the room as they whispered with uncertainty.

"Is that really what you want? All of you?" the Karchi woman asked, confused.

It was certainly an odd choice, but it was sadly fitting. We were made through dark means, and we were never going to be able to escape that fact, so we might as well accept it. I found myself nodding along with the rest of my siblings.

"Very well. Now, back to what I was saying, because we are unsure of your existence, we are requiring that you…Anathema, be supervised for the period of one year. You may go wherever and do whatever you please, but you will be watched to ensure that your souls are not corrupted. Is that agreeable to you?" the Karchi woman asked.

Again, most of my siblings and I nodded, but Ultha seemed annoyed by the idea. "We were told that we would be free from now on," Ultha remarked pointedly.

"You will be, of course, free. But you must undergo some supervision during your first year of freedom to ensure that you do not cause untold destruction. This is the best freedom we are willing to offer."

Ultha clicked her tongue and rolled her eyes, but after a moment she too nodded.

This time the Karchi woman smiled softly, and then gestured to everyone in the room. "Now, here is where I will ask for volunteers. Any council member, council employee, or guest may step up to take on this duty so long as they are prepared for the responsibility that comes alongside it."

The room was painfully silent, and I suddenly had the realization that this likely meant that I would be assigned to one of these volunteers and would never be able to see the blue-scaled man again. My mind felt like it stood on edge and I spun around once more to look toward the blue-scaled man. I wanted to look him in the eyes, to beg him to not let them take me away. But as I looked at him with wild eyes, he simply smiled, winked at me, and raised his hand as he cleared his throat.

"I would like to volunteer to take the candle gol-, I mean, Anathema. So long as she doesn't mind maybe having to go on an adventure or two with me that is," he smiled bashfully, as though realizing that I may not want to go with him at all for that very reason.

But I immediately turned back to the Karchi woman and blurted out the first word that came to mind. "Please!" I half-yelled, and the Karchi woman as well as many of the people in the room chuckled.

"I don't think there will be any objection to that arrangement." The Karchi woman smiled gently, and then continued the meeting, during which each of my siblings were assigned to different representatives or employees. Everyone was to go their separate ways with their separate chaperones, except for Ultha and Reeve who were assigned one chaperone after insisting on staying together.

Chapter 5:

Finding Home

At the end of the meeting as people began to disperse and exit the room, the blue-scaled man placed a gentle hand on my shoulder. I turned to face him, and he motioned for me to follow him. I did so quickly and obediently, not thinking to question where we were going. He began to lead me out of the room but stopped suddenly when someone called out a name.

"Luis! Come here for a moment please! You may bring your charge with you as well!" the voice said, and the blue-scaled man turned around to answer the call.

I carefully took a mental note. *His name is Luis, what a nice name.* I found myself smiling and followed after him as he went back further into the room and around the table. He stopped in front of the beautiful Karchi woman from before and stepped to the side, ushering me forward to stand beside him. I did so, and he placed a gentle hand on my back that sent shivers up my spine. I did my best not to show this reaction though, and simply smiled awkwardly at the woman before me.

"I'm sorry to call on you again, Luis, but I believe we have the matter of a reward to discuss." The woman smiled and Luis nodded. "Right, so obviously we can't give a reward for taking on the responsibility of your charge here, but we will be providing for them for this year via an allowance. And then of course there is the matter of the reward for your work for us, which after a charitable donation that I pulled some strings for, we can actually afford to give you." She chuckled nervously and unclipped a pouch from her side before handing it over to Luis. "I'll save you some trouble, there are six gold coins to provide for the girl, and-" she cleared her throat before continuing in a quieter voice as she leaned towards Luis. "Twenty gold coins for your services."

Luis and I both dropped our jaws in surprise. One of my chores before the closet days was to keep track of Firnyn's finances, so I knew how much money was worth. This amount was shocking to say the least as it equated to two hundred and sixty silver or twenty-six thousand copper. My portion, the six gold, was more than enough to take care of my expenses; provided that Luis didn't charge me rent that is. My stomach tightened as the thought of rent occurred to me, and after my mind raced for a moment, I forced myself to accept the probability that he would in fact charge me rent, and that I would need to budget very carefully the next year or until I could find a job.

Taking our shock in stride, the woman smiled and nodded before walking away, her many golden ornaments clinking as she walked. Luis quickly took the pack off his back, fumbling with his wings a bit to do so, and stuffed the pouch deep inside of it before re-securing it. He took a deep breath and turned to me. "Well, I certainly wasn't expecting a payout like that for a single job, but hey, pretty lucky!" he smiled wide, and patted me on the back before starting to walk away. "Oh!-" he stopped in his tracks and turned back to face me. "What should I call you by the way? Since you're now my 'charge' or whatever." He chuckled at the word and rolled his eyes.

I looked down at the ground, my cheeks warming as I said through a tight throat, "I was never gifted a name."

Luis put a hand to his chin and looked me up and down for a moment before shrugging. "I'll just call you 'kid' for now, and you can tell me your name when you decide on it. Ok?" I nodded, and giggled a bit as it occurred to me that he didn't look much older than me in regards to Human years.

With my temporary "name" in place, Luis nodded and once again motioned for me to follow him. He led me out of the room and a few paces forward over to a familiar hooded figure. I recognized him as the man that had held open the portal back at Firnyn's tower.

"Spookster!" Luis greeted him warmly and patted him on the shoulder. The man seemed less than thrilled to see Luis, but nodded and greeted him nonetheless. "So, I'm assuming you can take us back to my home now, right?" Luis asked, but in a way that seemed he already knew the answer would be 'yes.'

The man nodded once more, this time with a sarcastic smile, and moved over to the side of the hallway where he quickly began to cast what looked like a portal spell. Several minutes later, a light blue portal sprang forth from thin air and I looked at the man with admiration. Luis on the other hand took this in stride and simply strode through, stopping abruptly as he seemed to realize something.

"Thanks for everything Spookster. Maybe we'll see each other again one day." Luis gave the man a sloppy salute and waltzed through the portal.

I looked to the man, bowed slightly in thanks, and then ran through the portal. On the other side I ran face first into Luis's back, knocking him forward. He managed to right himself by catching a steady hand on the green couch next to us, and I quickly pushed myself off of him, my entire head burning as I felt my heart skip several beats. Luis chuckled and turned to face me. He then took my outstretched hand before bowing.

"I welcome you to my home, lady… kid?" He questioned himself as he spoke as he was unsure of how to address me. Then he straightened up and smiled. "Whatever, welcome home, kid. Feel free to make yourself comfy, and eat whatever you-" he stopped short as a thought occurred to him. "Do you eat?"

I nodded and held up one finger. "One candle a week."

His eyes widened and he put a hand on his chin. "Candles, huh? Well that's a new one. Though I guess it makes sense." He shrugged and held out his hands vertically and flat as though measuring something. "How big of a candle?" His hands were quite far apart so I hesitantly grabbed one of his hands and moved it closer to the other one, stopping when they were about six inches apart. He pouted his lower lip and nodded in understanding.

He stayed like this for a moment, and then seemed to remember I was there and stood up straight with his hands at his sides as he gave a guilty smile. "Anyway, get to know the place, I'm going to make some tea and then hit the hay. You can have the bedroom by the way, I'll take the couch," he said moving toward the kitchen, but once again stopped abruptly and turned to face me. "This may be a dumb question, but do you sleep?" he asked, his voice rising in pitch.

I smiled at his reactions and nodded. "I can sleep, but I don't have to."

"Good enough! So yeah you get the bedroom." He pointed at me, smiled, and made his way into the kitchen.

I took the chance to look around. On the left side was a fairly small living room with a couch, a simple coffee table, and four nicely made chairs with flower patterned cushions. The couch and chairs circled the coffee table, and behind this little seating area was a large window with flower patterned curtains. The living room connected to the kitchen through an open archway on the right side of the room and I could see Luis carefully retrieving a teacup from an intricately carved wooden and glass cabinet. He went to the water stone that sat next to the sink and held it over his cup before speaking its command word. I stared at him curiously, wondering how he was going to heat his tea, but saw that all of a sudden, his water was steaming in his cup. I cautiously walked into the kitchen and cleared my throat.

"How did you do that? Do you know magic?" I asked, pointing to the cup.

"Hm? Oh, yeah. It's the only bit of magic I know, so I always keep the runes on me." He proved this by setting down his cup to unclip his pauldron and show that he had the runes Algiz (the utility rune) and the water and fire runes carved into the leather of a band he wore around his arm. "Way more helpful than you'd think actually." He smiled and began putting sugar cubes into his cup.

He added about eight cubes, and I wondered how he could drink his tea so sweet, though at the same time it dawned on me that I had never drunk tea before. At least not in this life. I chalked it up to be one of the random memories I had from my life as Firnyn's sister, and found myself shrugging at the thought. Luis noticed this and smiled a bit wider before carrying his cup towards me. I quickly moved out of the way to allow him to pass and he slipped by to go sit on the couch. He sat down heavily, causing air to rush out from the cushion as it was squished, and he took a long sniff of his tea, settling into the crevice he had made. I watched him closely, taking mental note of what chores I would likely be

42

assigned such as making him tea and cleaning the cups afterwards. It occurred to me that the entire place could also use a thorough dusting as I noticed several shelves with a thick layer of dust on them. I glanced around for the cleaning supplies as I stood there, but there were none in sight. I was wondering to myself where they could be, and what lay through the door at the far end of the room when Luis turned around, an arm propped up on the back of the couch.

"Are you gonna sit? Or?" he asked hesitantly, his eyes darting to the sides.

My eyes widened, I had never been allowed to sit while Firnyn was in the room, and I had instinctively assumed it would be the same with Luis. I smiled at my stupidity and made my way over to one of the chairs where I sat down carefully. For several moments, we sat in silence as Luis sipped his tea with his eyes closed as though he was enjoying the warmth it brought him. Then as he finished his cup, he placed it gently on the coffee table and looked over to me.

"So, I'm guessing you don't really want to talk about how things were back there with that Firnyn guy?" he asked, though it sounded more like a question that he was sure of the answer for.

I simply nodded. The thought of explaining my predicament and the years I spent in it made my chest hurt, and I knew that talking about it would only make it worse. Luis took my response in stride and simply began to tell me stories about himself. He talked for about an hour, detailing two particularly gruesome stories that he had prevailed through and come out a better person for it at the end; or that was how he put it anyway. I listened intently, captivated both by his skillful storytelling and the way he moved as he spoke. By the time he was done I was so enraptured by the story that I had completely forgotten the time. Luis seemed tired to say the least, and he went through the door on the far end of the room and opened a small closet door that sat on the other side in the hallway. He grabbed several blankets and pillows and began piling them on the couch, building his little "nest" as he had called it. As he finished, he motioned for me to follow him and led me a little way down the hallway where there were two doors, both open. The door on the right was a bathroom, containing only the bare necessities, and on the left was the bedroom. Inside, Luis had mounted several 'trophies' on the walls: keys, pelts, ribbons, and more.

Luis nodded in approval as he looked around the room. "Yep, this is my prized collection from the best battles and challenges I've ever faced. Brings a tear to my eye just thinking about it," he joked, raising the pitch of his voice and miming at wiping away a tear.

I smiled and moved into the room, taking a seat on the bed and looking back out the door to where Luis still stood.

"Let me know if you need anything. I'll be right on the couch." Luis patted the door frame twice before slowly closing the door.

Once Luis's footsteps faded away, I sighed heavily; it had been a very eventful day. With this in mind, I curled up onto the bed. It was the first time I had been in a bed in three years, and I fell right to sleep.

Chapter 6:

A Closet is a Girl's Best Friend

The day after the kid joined my little slice of paradise, I had intended to start my morning like I always did; by making myself tea and breakfast. But, when I sleepily wandered into the kitchen, I found the kid there cooking eggs. My first reaction was admittedly to wide-eyed point at her as though she were a marvel of nature. Though I suppose she was a marvel of nature, but that's beside the point. I was about to open my mouth to question her, but she took the words right out of my mouth.

"I know I said I don't eat, but I know how to cook. So, I made you breakfast," she said with a smile.

I lowered my hand and bashfully rubbed the back of my head. "Aw, you didn't have to do that."

"Yes, I did? This is part of my chores from now on, right?" she asked in confusion, but she skillfully kept her hands moving so as not to burn the eggs.

"Chores? What are you talking about?"

"I'm expected to do chores while I live here, right? So, I'm making breakfast, and I dusted the living room and wiped down the kitchen. I'll make your tea in a second, and then while you eat I'll mop the floors," she said matter-of-factly, as though nothing were wrong with it.

"Kid, you *don't* have to do chores. In fact, you're my guest, so you shouldn't be doing anything at all!" I walked over to her and put a hand on her shoulder. "Listen, I don't know what life was for you back there, but here? Here you relax and enjoy what the world has to offer. So, no, you aren't expected to do chores."

The kid looked like I had stabbed her or something by saying that, and carefully set down the skillet to the side. She then began to walk away, head hung. I started to say something, but became more curious about where she was going to go. I peeked out of the kitchen archway, and saw her open the door to the hallway. *No, she wouldn't. Would she?* I said to myself as a thought occurred to me. Just as I had suspected, she walked into the hall closet and shut the door behind her. I sighed, walking over to the closet door. I hesitated to open it, not wanting to upset her even more, and opted to just talk to her.

"Kid, you know you're free now. You don't have to be in closets anymore, ever again! Please come out." My voice was tight and warbled with worry.

I heard some light rustling, and then the door slowly opened. The kid stood there, tears perched in her bright purple eyes, and fiddled with her hands as she was trying to say something. Eventually I was able to catch a few words. "I don't know what else to do," she muttered, keeping her head lowered in shame.

I took a gentle hand under her chin and forced her to look up at me. I smiled at her. "All you have to do is relax. Let me worry about everything else," I said, and dropped my hand from her.

She gave a weak smile and swiped away her tears before responding. "I appreciate that you'd let me stay here without doing chores, but I've never really relaxed before. At least, I don't think so. I mean there were times where I was allowed to be idle, so I guess if you consider that relaxing?"

I crossed my arms and tried to keep my cool as a fiery anger flashed through me. *Damn that bastard, Firnyn. What the hell did he do to her?* I thought and cleared my throat as the kid stared up at me patiently. "Right, well, what did you do when you were 'idle'?" I put air quotes around the word.

The kid thought for a moment, her eyes darting down as she did so, and then replied sadly, "I...I guess I talked to Ultha and Reeve..."

She seemed to be pained with memories, so I quickly clapped my hands. "Good, ok. Well you have me, so we can talk whenever you'd like." I smiled wide, trying to cheer her up. "Anything else, though?"

She smiled at my offer, and then thought again for a moment to answer my question. "Well, before Ultha and Reeve were made, I suppose I just looked out the window at the meadow. I always wanted to see those flowers up close," she admitted.

"Wait, we went through that meadow when you first left the tower. Why didn't you stop and look at them?"

"You seemed like you were in a hurry, so I didn't want to bother you." She spoke in a hushed voice, as though this too brought her shame.

"Kid! No! You are seriously lacking in the common sense department." I chuckled at first, but she made a pained face, and I realized I had offended her. "Wait, that's not what I meant! I just

47

mean to say that the life you had before now taught you all the wrong stuff," I panicked to explain, but then sighed and shook my head. "Listen, you are your own person, so next time if you're following me and you want to stop for something, then we're stopping. And that's final." I smiled again and went to put a hand on top of her head. I stopped short of this, though, as I realized that she didn't have hair to be ruffled, since it was made of wax, and that there was a candle wick in the way on her head. I slipped my hand on her shoulder instead.

The kid smiled sweetly, warming my heart, and I nodded in approval before moving along. "So, you like flowers, huh? Well, I think you're going to find that we're quite alike in that aspect." I held my head up proudly.

She looked at me questioningly, so I motioned for her to follow. I led her out the front door and around toward the back of the house where there lay a large garden containing both flowers and produce. I heard the kid gasp, and turned around to see that she stared at it in awe. I chuckled. "I've always loved gardening. It's tough work, but the results are worth it. It's actually one of the ways I relax," I explained and knelt down next to some daisies I had growing.

The kid quickly followed suit and knelt down beside me, her eyes practically sparkling as she looked at the small buds. I caressed one of the buds, careful not to break any petals, and smiled as I felt its softness. I caught myself soon after, and blushed, retrieving my hand. "I know, not exactly the hobby you'd think of a great adventurer having. But…well I-" I was struggling to explain, but dropped short as I realized that the kid was paying zero attention to me, and was instead carefully caressing the daisy just as I had done. After she had touched it, she looked up at me and smiled. I lost all embarrassment and smiled right back at her.

48

She glanced away after a moment and mumbled, "Would you teach me?"

"About gardening? Yeah, of course! Maybe it will teach you what relaxing is all about." I was thrilled at the idea, happy to have someone else that liked flowers as much as me.

We spent most of the morning going over each of the plants in the garden and how to tend to them. By the time we were done, the sun was high in the sky, beating its rays down upon us. I looked over to the kid, ready to ask her if she wanted to go back inside when I noticed something drip onto her shoulder. Thinking at was from a bird, I quickly swiped it off of her, not wanting to gross her out. It stuck to my hand a bit and I went to wipe it off on my pant leg when I realized that it was beginning to harden. My mind raced in disgust as I wondered what kind of bird this could've been, when it dawned on me that it was candle wax and the kid's wax hair was melting.

"Oh dear gods, you're melting! Come on!" I scooped her up into a princess carry and ran to the front door. I fumbled for a moment with the door handle, but soon opened it and rushed inside. I set her down carefully on the couch and then rushed to the hall closet where, after some digging, I retrieved the biggest candle I could find and a small folding fan. I rushed back in the room, and shoved the candle into her hands as I began to rapidly fan her. My gut reaction seemed to pay off as the wax hair returned to a hardened state, and the kid began munching on the candle I had given her. It made a small crunching sound with each bite that served to remind me that she was eating a *candle* of all things. The idea of it sent shivers up my spine, but I did my best to not show her this; I didn't want her to feel like she was weird for simply eating.

49

A few moments later, she had finished her candle, and I saw the places near the wick that had melted off slowly began to materialize back as though they were fading back into existence. I stared in awe for a moment, but caught myself as she looked up at me curiously. I smiled awkwardly and moved around to the front of the couch to sit next to her. The cushion made a gasping sound as my weight plopped onto it, and I cleared my throat as I thought of what to say.

"So you melt, huh? That must be really difficult to deal with," I started, but immediately wanted to apologize as it felt like the stupidest thing I could've said.

She didn't seem to mind, though, and nodded. "If it gets over one hundred degrees and if I'm in direct sunlight, then I'll begin to melt. I don't know what happens if I melt all the way, though."

"Well let's not find out." I patted her on the back, and then leaned my head back onto the back of the couch. "I need a nap. You should work on relaxing while I sleep, just look out the window, read a book, anything. But no cleaning!" I warned her.

She nodded and stood up so I could lay out on the couch. I fell right to sleep, and assumed she would go back to the bedroom to relax. But, when I awoke about an hour later from a deep growling in my stomach, I found the kid standing still in the same place she was before I fell asleep. She appeared to be looking out the window, but when she noticed me stir, she turned her attention towards me.

"Were…were you standing there the whole time?" I stared at her with wide eyes in disbelief.

"Yes. I was looking out the window like you told me to do. Well, and I watched over you while you slept. You know you snore, by the way," she said nonchalantly.

I mimed with two fingers, as though showing something becoming smaller. "Ok, you need to relax on the creepy factor here, kid."

"Creepy?" her voice squeaked as she made a pained face.

I instantly felt awful for calling her that. "Sorry, I wasn't thinking. I didn't mean to call you creepy. Just, try not to do anymore 'watching over me', ok?"

She nodded sadly, and turned to start walking towards the hallway.

"And no going back in the closet!" I scolded her gently, and she froze in place before sheepishly turning back around.

Just then my stomach growled loudly, and she seemingly instinctively went into the kitchen. I sighed and followed behind her, watching as she cleaned up the eggs from that morning and began to make sandwiches. I let her work for a few moments until she noticed me. She once again froze in place like she was a criminal caught in the act. I chuckled and rubbed the back of my head.

"Listen kid, I just don't want you to feel like you have to do chores and take care of me, but if you want to do a few chores here and there I won't stop you."

The kid nodded happily and with a skip in her step, went back to preparing the sandwiches. The rest of the day I spent reading, and she spent cleaning the house from top to bottom. She obliged me a few times to rest on the couch next to me, but for the most part she kept busy. It was an hour before sunset and everything was starting to cool off, which meant it was time for my daily workout. By this point the kid had made the house spotless, and was fidgeting quietly with her hands as she stared out the window. I sighed, a little frustrated that she didn't know how to relax, but then a thought occurred to me. *Who knows how often and for how long she was trapped in that closet by Firnyn. Poor thing must've been dying to do something, anything except sit in the dark.* My heart ached deeply at this, and I felt regret for scolding her initially. I got up from the couch, and walked over to her, kneeling down beside the chair where she sat.

"Kid, would you like to come join me for my work out? You can train with me or just watch, but it'll be good to get you out of the house. Here, you can have my book in case you want to read," I offered, and she gently took the book, looking at it like a prize she had won.

She then hugged it to her chest and stood up alongside me. We went out the door and into the open field where my house sat, over to a small training ground I had constructed decades ago. It had a small running track, dumbbells, training dummy, and punching bag, all positioned around the tree in the center of the circular track. I wasn't practicing swordplay that day, so my work out today would consist of running, pushups, situps, and finally a few rounds with the punching bag. The kid walked to the tree and sat beneath it before opening the book and starting to read. I, on the other hand, began my warmup stretches and prepared for my run. We both did our tasks diligently, and as the sun's rays were turning the sky pink with sunset, I finished mine. I looked over to the kid who still sat reading, the only proof that she had moved at all during that time being the book was open to farther along in the story.

52

I placed a gentle hand on the back of her head so as not to disturb her wick, and spoke through heavy breaths, "Time to head back, kid. Before it gets too dark out."

She nodded silently, and stood, clinging the book to her chest once more. After dinner that night, I told her some more stories of my adventures before we both hit the hay.

Chapter 7:

Shopping Trip

A few days passed during my time with Luis, and we had settled into a routine. He allowed me to do the chores, and he either read, gardened, or packed and repacked his bag with various adventuring gear. When I asked why he fiddled with the pack so much, he replied that he always wanted to be prepared. This didn't make much sense to me, but I took it at face value and continued along in my day.

It was after these few days that Luis decided that we should go on a shopping trip, and hurried to get his things before pushing me out the door. This didn't bother me, though the risk of melting again did, and I gently reminded him of it.

"Ok, stay right there!" He smiled and ran back in the house. A moment passed and he had returned with a thick quilt in his hands, which he threw around me and over my head like a cowl.

I felt like a grandma wearing it, and apparently, I looked like it as Luis stifled a laugh. I hung my head as my cheeks grew hot. "Oh no, no, no! It's fine. You look fine! I didn't mean to laugh. I'm sorry," he scrambled to apologize.

His frantic reaction made me smile, and seeing this, he relaxed and sighed heavily. We both chuckled at this, and then we set out on our journey. The walk to the nearest village took about two hours, and as the morning continued to grow ever hotter, I silently thanked myself for thinking to remind Luis. We arrived in the village a little before noon and found that it was bustling with activity. It was a fairly small village, but still had lots of people moving through its main street. "Why are there so many people here? There's no way this small of a village fits all of them."

"The village sits on a major trade route between two cities, so there's constantly lots of people moving in and out of here," he explained over the crowd's noise.

I nodded, and looked at the people around me. Many of them gave me strange looks, but others seemed to not notice me at all. Luis guided me through the crowd, but stopped once he had gotten to what appeared to be the village market. Assuming he had come for groceries, I was surprised when he walked us over to a clothing shop. There were clothes of several types, though all appeared to be very well made. At the back of the shop sat a horned man with bright white hair and slight fangs. I assumed him to be an Adarra, or horned Demon, but was surprised when he came out from behind the counter as he was in fact a Sky Lamia, half-Human half-snake humanoids that can fly. This shocked me, as Sky Lamias were known to be nomadic, never staying in one place for more than six months at a time. The man slithered forward towards Luis, and greeted him with a hug.

"Luis! Welcome back! How can I help you today?" He only addressed Luis, seemingly not having noticed me yet.

"Yeah, I'm looking for a new dress for the kid. Oh and a big veil that will block out the sun please." He motioned over his shoulder to me with a thumb, and the man looked at me with wide eyes. "You ok, Cyrus?" Luis asked when he didn't respond.

"Hm? Oh, yes, of course. Does she need to be fitted for one, or do you know her measurements?" Cyrus kept his eyes locked on Luis, as though refusing to acknowledge me again.

Luis rubbed a hand on his chin in thought. "I mean I could take a guess…No, better not. Just fit her for one please."

"Of course. And do you have a style in mind?"

"Yeah, something light so she doesn't heat up too much, and something on the shorter side so she can work in the garden if she wants." Luis hurried that last part a little as he likely realized that him asking for a shorter dress for me would be misconstrued.

Cyrus nodded and instructed me to get on a small circular platform that had a mirror positioned in front of it. I looked up to Luis, unsure if I should do as Cyrus said, but Luis gave me a small wink and motioned for me to do so. I swallowed hard and stepped up onto the platform. Cyrus grabbed a tape measure and walked over to me, but then hesitated as he looked at my dress.

"Gods, Luis. Did you clothe her in literal rags?" he said in disappointment.

"What? No! I mean, *I* didn't do anything. Just, please make her a new one," Luis fumbled through his words and ended with a quiet, meek voice as though asking forgiveness.

Cyrus shook his head while clicking his tongue, but turned back to me nonetheless. He then carefully held the tape measure up to and around different parts of my body. A few moments later, he slithered over to his desk where he scribbled down a bunch of numbers, which I assumed to be the measurements, and instructed me to step down from the platform. I hopped down and returned to my place beside Luis while he talked to Cyrus. Cyrus still seemed perturbed by the fact that I was wearing such ragged clothing and gave several glares as Luis tried to explain himself. In the end, Cyrus shooed us out of the shop with a promise that the dress would be done by the end of the day.

"Well, next on the agenda is shoes. I'm guessing being barefoot doesn't bother you, but it worries me, so we're getting you some shoes." Luis said as though his mind couldn't be changed.

I nodded, though I felt my heart droop like a cut flower as I realized something. "You're spending my portion of the money, right? Not your portion?"

Luis gave a guilty smile and rubbed the back of his head. "Well, you caught me. Yeah I'm using my money. Consider it a thank you gift for doing so much for me the past few days."

My pulse increased rapidly. "A gift. I've never...Thank you." I spoke softly but gave a genuine smile to which Luis patted me on the back.

"Let's get to getting, kid. To the cobbler!" Luis pointed a finger to a building down the road and started forward.

I giggled at his enthusiasm, and followed quickly after him. We arrived a few moments later at a small shop, much smaller than the clothing shop had been. Inside, the door hit a bell as it opened, which made a small chime. The cobbler, a Gnome, was sitting by the counter in the back of the store resting his head on the wood of it, as he was fast asleep.

Seeing this, Luis called out in a loud voice, "Arjen! You wonderful bastard, wake up and greet your friend!"

Arjen woke with a start, drool dripping down his chin and his large mouse ears standing straight up in surprise. "Oh, hello

Luis. Did you tear through your soles again?" he said sleepily as he grabbed a nearby hat into which he carefully tucked his ears.

Luis chuckled sheepishly. "No...though I'll probably need some new boots at some point. Make me an extra pair when you have a free day, would you?"

Arjen wiped his chin with the sleeve of his blue jacket and hopped down from his stool before wandering out to the front of the counter. The counter no longer hiding them, we could now see his large feet which were almost as long as he was tall and wearing two very nicely made black shoes. He walked much closer than I anticipated as he bent down to look at my feet, dirtied with mud and dust from the walk here.

Arjen tilted his head and made a groaning sound. "I'm not sure I have anything small enough. These feet are the size of a child's. The shoes you want are for this, correct?" he said peering up at Luis.

Luis nodded, and Arjen walked back behind the counter and into a door that had been cut out in the larger door that was back there. We waited patiently as we heard rummaging coming from the other side of the door, until finally Arjen returned carrying a small box. He hopped up onto his stool and slid the box across the counter toward Luis.

"I'm not sure they'll fit. They may be a little big, but they're the best I have for the moment. You can have these for fifty copper, and it'll be another fifty copper to make the new pair. You're wanting boots, yes?"

Luis nodded again and started to pull the coins out from his coin purse. Then he tapped it to the counter once, twice, three times before he placed it on the counter and grabbed the box.

58

Bending down, he opened the box and revealed a small pair of brown boots. Luis took out one at a time and wrapped a hand around one of my ankles as a way to let me know he would put the boots on for me. I flushed with warmth, but carefully lifted my foot nonetheless. I had to put a hand onto one of his shoulders to steady myself, but Luis didn't seem to mind, and slipped the boot onto my foot. I placed my foot back down and wiggled my toes, getting a feel for the boot, and realized that they were in fact a little big. But I didn't say anything since they wouldn't impede my walking or anything. Luis put the next boot on me as well and I looked down at the boots, then up to him as he stood. He gave me a thumbs up and a questioning face, and I nodded and smiled in response.

Arjen waved us off as we left the store, and I stopped after just leaving to look to Luis. "Thank you. I really do appreciate it," I said with my cheeks burning.

Luis smiled and put a gentle hand on my shoulder. "Any time, kid. Now let's go get some groceries!" he made his voice sound deep and bellowing like an announcer at a joust as he said the last part.

I giggled and followed after him as he led me toward the grocery market. It was much further down the main road, and off to one side. As we walked I kept my eyes glued to Luis's back, not wanting to lose sight of him, especially as we got into the market area itself. The market was packed with people that buzzed around the different stalls like flies. We started by going to a bag vendor to get all of the bags we'd need to carry everything, and then started our shopping. We went up to several stalls, but no matter what stall we went to, everyone knew Luis's name. No one noticed me as they were enthralled by Luis's presence. Luis didn't stay at any one stall for too long, but with the number of people that wanted to

59

stop and talk to him, it took us well over three hours to get all of our groceries.

After we had bought everything, Luis decided to make a stop at another shop, the candle maker. We headed across the street from the market into the candle shop, where there sat an elderly Human woman. As Luis talked with her, I found myself touching at the wax of my arm as I wondered if, despite all odds, I too would grow old one day. Luis went around the shop and began grabbing as many candles as he could reasonably fit in one of our large cloth bags when the old woman suggested that he just buy two of her boxes of candles, which would total at around one hundred candles. Luis loved the idea, and immediately bought three boxes instead.

Carrying his three large boxes in his hands with several bags of groceries hanging on his arms, Luis walked down the street with a wide gait. I, on the other hand, only carried one bag since I had to use the other hand to hold the blanket on my head. I felt a strange sensation of a pain in my heart at the thought that I was a burden to Luis, and my mind swirled around this sentiment until Luis arrived at his destination. We had walked into a small shop that was full to the brim with flowers of various kinds. As we walked in, Luis sat down his items over in a corner and began to peruse the shop. There didn't appear to be a shopkeeper, though, and I was going to question him on this when I heard a voice from behind us.

"Luis Rockwell, as I live and breathe. What are you doing in my little shop?" A Wood Elf woman with long brown hair that she let flow around her walked into the shop and marched right up to Luis.

"Oh, Juli h-how are y-you?" Luis stuttered, clearly flustered as I could see a flash of red under his scales from how embarrassed and nervous he was.

I furrowed my brow and tilted my head to the side as I thought. I hadn't known Luis very long, but he didn't seem like the type to get this flustered. I didn't understand what Juli had done to make him act that way, but I shrugged it off as I listened to their conversation.

"I'm doing just fine, dear. And how are you?" Juli asked smoothly, clearly not as affected as Luis.

"G-Good. I...I'd like to get a bouquet please," Luis said hurriedly.

From there they proceeded to 'talk shop' as they discussed the best flowers for decorating Luis's house. While they did so, I wandered around the shop looking at all the flowers and stopping to smell a few. But then, my eye caught on a particular flower, a white rose. I set my bag down on the ground as I cupped one in my hands and carefully smelled its gentle scent. For some reason this flower filled me with the urge to run and jump and spin, and I found myself staring intently at it. I stayed like this for a moment until their conversation caught my attention once more.

"Oh, by the way. I didn't know you got a golem! Must be helpful around the house. That one does seem a little odd though." Juli chuckled and punched Luis gently on the arm.

My entire being filled with an icky black feeling, something that began to eat me alive inside, and I grabbed my bag and ran outside, not waiting to hear Luis's response. *That's all I am to them? A tool? A slave?* I screamed in my head, and began to run faster, dodging through the crowd of people dexterously. I ran down the street and found myself back at the tailor. Without thinking, I opened the door and curled up in one corner of the room, clinging my knees to my chest. There was no closet here, no place for guaranteed safety, but this was the best I could do. I shook with tears as I heard Cyrus move towards me and put a hand on my shoulder. He didn't say anything, but his presence was comforting, and I soon managed to pull myself together. As I wiped the last of my tears away, Luis came sprinting through the door, gasping for air as he stopped inside and kneeled down on the floor. He took a moment to catch his breath, and then he wiggled his way forward on the ground until he was face to face with me.

"She didn't know. Most people aren't going to know. But you have to be strong, and know in your heart that you're freaking fantastic, kid. You're not just a golem," he said earnestly and then put a gentle hand on my cheek, gave it a squeeze, and released it.

Luis scooted back and stood up, offering me a hand. I took it and he pulled me to my feet in one swift motion. He explained gently that he left the groceries and candles behind and that he would have to go get them. He instructed me to stay put while he did so, so he wouldn't lose me. My cheeks grew warm at this, and I did as he said, walking around the store as I waited. Cyrus went back to sewing as I looked around, and only glanced up every now and then to look at me. I figured this was either his way of checking on me, or his way of ensuring I didn't run off. About twenty minutes passed, when Cyrus stood up from his seat and grabbed the garment he had been sewing off of the table. He held it up to the light, nodded, and carried it over to me.

"Here you go. We have a changing room behind that curtain," he said, handing the dress to me.

I didn't look at it much as I put it on, wanting to keep it a surprise for myself when I walked in front of the mirror. Then, I quickly walked out and stepped onto the platform nervously, unsure of how I'd look. The beige dress was perfect, with a sturdy leather corset sewn on top and the rest of it made of incredibly soft fabric that puffed out at the sleeves and skirt. Cyrus came over and began to help me tighten and tie the corset, as I had done a sloppy job of doing so in my hurry. The dress, now properly tied, looked even better than before, and my heart soared as I did a little spin in front of the mirror. When I had finished my spin, I heard the door open, and I expectantly leaned to get a better look at the entrance. My expectations were correct, as it was Luis who waddled in carrying all of the bags and boxes. He set them down with a huff and turned to look toward us. As he saw me, for a moment his jaw went slack and his eyes wide. But he quickly composed himself and cleared his throat in embarrassment.

"Looks good, kid. You ready to go?" he said, trying to pretend he hadn't had the reaction he did.

I giggled and nodded, hopping down from the platform, and quickly moving to his side. Luis gave me a gentle pat on the back and then grabbed his pouch to pay Cyrus for the dress. Luis tried to do the transaction without me hearing the price, but I overheard anyway, instantly feeling my throat close as I found out that he was paying three whole silver for my dress. I tried to protest as I heard this, insisting that Luis pay with my portion of the money. But he wasn't having any of that and grabbed my face with one hand, squishing my cheeks.

"No, and that's final," he said sternly, but then immediately winked as he let go and turned back to Cyrus.

My head felt like it was going to float off my body when he did that, and I tried desperately to compose myself while Luis paid.

"Oh, and here's this. It's what we give to vampires." Cyrus handed Luis a folded piece of sheer fabric.

Luis took it, and moved to grab for his coin pouch again. But Cyrus touched his arm and shook his head, insisting that it was free. Luis was about to argue, but Cyrus raised his eyebrows and tilted his head, giving him a look of warning and insistence. Luis sighed, grabbed our things, and we began walking home. I opted not to wear the veil on the walk, since it would be dark before long. On our walk, though, something occurred to me, and I hesitantly asked Luis about it.

"Luis, why don't you just fly to and from town? Wouldn't it be faster?" I asked timidly.

"Oh, I usually do, but I wanted to take you with me. Plus, I can't carry you and everything else. I'd drop something and I don't want that to be you," he chuckled.

The rest of the walk home, we chatted every now and then, but mostly it was spent in a comfortable silence. By the time we got home, it was three hours after sunset, and after making Luis some dinner, we promptly went to sleep in our respective spots.

Chapter 8:

Tranquility Under the Summer Sun

Several days passed slowly, but happily. It did come to a point a few times, though, where I was recleaning the same thing, knowing that I wouldn't have anything to do after I had finished with it. I think Luis caught on to my boredom, and he would often offer to garden with me. I took him up on this every time, as I loved practicing my gardening, plus having him guide me made the process much more enjoyable. I figured that this was what he would ask when he approached me one morning, but instead, he asked if I wanted to go on a picnic. In my surprise, I nodded without thinking, and found myself being whisked away. After packing a quick lunch for himself and a candle for me, he practically pushed me out the door. I unfurled my veil outside, ready to begin the walk to wherever he wanted to go, when Luis suddenly scooped me up in his arms into a princess carry. I clutched onto my veil just as he spread his wings wide and, with a whoosh of air, flew into the sky.

Luis flew surprisingly fast, and it only took a few minutes to arrive at a small lake with weeping willow trees huddled around its edges. As Luis landed, his wings kicking up some dust from their large wingbeats, I pushed myself out of his grasp and teetered a bit as I stepped back on solid ground. I felt Luis's arms grab me under my own arms, and I looked back to smile at him. I was still a bit shaken, but I had also never flown before, making it a unique experience. Looking at the sea of grass race by was breathtaking, and part of me wanted to go flying with him again.

But none of that mattered when I saw what was in the lake. Swimming in a line near one edge of the water was a family of ducks. I had never seen a duck in person before, only in pictures, and hearing their small quacks as they communicated to one another filled my heart with warmth. I had apparently been staring at them a bit too intently as I heard Luis chuckle behind me.

"You can feed them some of my bread if you want," he offered, pulling out the loaf from the bag he had packed.

It felt like my eyes would jump out of my head from excitement as I nodded fervently. Luis chuckled once more and ripped off a piece of the loaf before handing the piece to me. I approached the ducks slowly, not wanting to scare them off and stopped a good distance away. I then ripped off a tiny piece of bread and tossed it into the water. At first, this scared them, and the ducklings quacked loudly as they swam away from it. But the mother duck seemed to know exactly what it was and went for it immediately. Seeing their mother eat the bread, the ducklings were much less nervous when I threw the next piece in, and they quickly swarmed around it, trying to be the first to eat. I smiled watching this, happy that they seemed happy as well. I did this for a few minutes until I ran out of bread and turned around to look to Luis. Luis had set out a blanket and was eating some of his bread slowly as he watched me with amusement. Now out of the shade of the willow trees, I threw the veil over my head so I wouldn't risk melting, and walked over to Luis, eyebrow raised.

"What?" I asked, confused as to why he was so interested in what I was doing.

"Nothin'," Luis said through a mouthful of bread as he looked up and to the left.

I shrugged and sat down beside him as he handed me my candle. I tucked it up inside the veil so I could reach my mouth, and slowly began to crunch into it with my teeth. The first time I ever ate a candle, back in my days with Firnyn, I hated the texture of the waxy crumbles as they filled my mouth. But, as time went on, I grew accustomed to it to the point that I couldn't imagine eating anything else. They didn't have a taste to me, though, which made the process always a bit lackluster since I seemed to have memory of tastes I must have experienced in my past life. I looked out at the lake and reclined back on one hand as I watched the light dance off its waters. Luis had moved on to eating some jerky, and followed my example, leaning back onto one hand as he too stared out at the lake. We relaxed like this for about an hour, occasionally chatting, but mostly just taking in the scenery. When we were done, Luis packed up the blanket while I waved goodbye to the ducks who didn't seem to remember that I existed at all. I smiled as a gentle hollow feeling filled my stomach and I turned back to face Luis.

"Ready?" Luis asked and held out his arms as though implying that he would carry me, and we would fly back. I nodded and let him scoop me up before we flew back home.

The next day, Luis surprised me once again with an activity for the day, shopping in town. I was confused, as we weren't yet out of groceries, but decided to hold my tongue and go along anyway. Since we weren't going to be carrying much, Luis decided we would fly there, so after I put on my veil, we began the about twenty-minute flight to town. When we arrived, we landed just outside of town, so we wouldn't draw too much attention to ourselves, and walked in on the main street.

Luis guided me through town over to a small store that sat next to Cyrus's clothing store. It had a sign with a ball of yarn engraved on it, and I looked up at Luis, curious as to why we were there. Luis caught sight of my confused look, and turned simply offering a wink in return before heading into the store. Inside, there were shelves and shelves full of yarn, and one section specifically for looms and knitting needles. Luis grabbed a bag off of his back and began throwing in balls of yarn left and right, seemingly on a mission to grab one of every color. He grabbed as many as he could fit before moving over to the implements section and grabbing one set of every size they had. I watched in a mix of curiosity and confusion, unsure what he planned to do with so much knitting supplies. Luis then took the bag to the front counter where he emptied everything onto it in front of a young Cetan woman, a hawk-winged person, who began to tally everything together on a piece of paper, and write down a total price. Luis promptly paid the woman, and scooped everything back into the bag before turning back to me with a wide smile on his face.

"Let's get to gettin'!" Luis said as he moved past me and out the door. I followed him closely as he headed down the street, and a few paces in the direction of the outskirts of town, he stopped. "Do you enjoy candles with scents added to them more than regular candles? Like would a strawberry scented candle taste like strawberries to you?" He asked, peering over his shoulder at me.

I noticed some people getting frustrated at Luis stopping in the middle of the moving crowd, and gently grabbed him by the corner of his shirt and led him over to the side of the road that the crowd didn't touch as they moved. He chuckled and repeated the question.

"I don't know. I've never had a scented candle before." I shrugged thinking that would be the end of it, but he grabbed my hand in his and began leading me toward the candle shop, I assumed. My heart beat rapidly as we walked, and I couldn't tell if it was because of our quickened pace or the warmth from his hand in mine. My assumption was correct as we walked into the candle shop. There was another patron in the shop, but they left soon after we entered, leaving us alone with the shopkeeper.

"Luis! Welcome back my dear," the old woman greeted Luis. "Surely you can't already be out of candles? What is it that you need from me today?"

"I'm looking for some scented candles, actually. Maybe some fruity ones or sweet-scented ones," Luis explained.

The old woman hobbled out from behind the counter with her cane and walked over to one of the shelves. "I recommend anything on this shelf." She pointed with her cane and then shuffled back behind the counter.

Luis grabbed a few candles off the shelf, smelling each one before adding them to the bag. He paid for them at the counter, and we walked out into the street where Luis led us over to a bench. He then handed me one of the scented candles, and motioned for me to try it. I hesitantly cracked into it, unsure if the taste would be bad or not, but was pleasantly surprised as my mouth filled with a gentle sweetness. There was another taste as well, something bitter that rested in the back of the mouth, but the sweetness made this easy to ignore. I happily munched on the candle for a little while as Luis watched me intently. I smiled up at him and gave him a thumbs up as I continued to eat. This seemed to satisfy Luis's curiosity and he simply began to watch the people in the crowd pass by. When I had finished, Luis patted me on the back and motioned for me to follow him. I followed along obediently until I saw that he was taking us to the flower shop. I stopped in my tracks as he walked up to the door, and my throat felt like it was closing as my head spun.

Luis walked over to me and knelt down in front of me, taking my hand in his. "Hey, you remember what I said, right? She just didn't know. But I explained it to her, so now she does. She's a good person. She won't treat you like that again."

My stomach swirled, but I nodded nonetheless as I stared at the store. Luis nodded back, and stood, keeping my hand in his as he guided me into the store. Inside, Juli was behind the counter reading with her feet propped up on the counter when we walked in, and at first she merely glanced up at us, keeping her attention mostly on her book. But as she saw that it was us, she put a bookmark inside the book and sat up properly, putting her feet down on the ground. She looked nervous, as well as a little guilty. Luis gave a bumbling greeting, and she stood and walked out from behind the counter before hesitantly walking over to me. I instinctively tried to hide behind Luis, but he stepped out of the way to let her see me. My face flushed and I felt dizzy and a little sick, unsure of what she would say and how I would handle it.

"Hey…I'm…I'm sorry about the other day. I never would've…I mean I shouldn't have…well, you know what I mean." She chuckled awkwardly and offered me a hand. "Friends?"

I looked from her hand to her face a few times, unsure of what to do, but then Luis elbowed me gently in the side. I glanced up at him and he widened his eyes and motioned from me to her with them. I turned my head back to Juli who stood there still wearing a sad smile and holding out her hand, and I carefully placed my hand in hers. She instantly brightened and smiled wide before releasing my hand from her hold and turning to look at Luis.

"So, what brings you back so soon? You didn't already kill that bouquet I gave you, did you?" Juli teased him and pinched one of his cheeks between her fingers.

Luis began to turn so red that I could easily see it from under his scales, and rubbed the back of his head awkwardly as Juli continued to tease him, seemingly oblivious to how flustered Luis

70

was getting. Luis eventually took a deep breath and changed the topic from Juli's jesting.

"A-Anyway, I was wondering, and now you don't have to if you don't want to, but I'd really appreciate it if you could...Could you teach us how to knit?" he asked as he pulled the bag off his back to show Juli his haul of supplies.

Juli rummaged through the bag and began to giggle. "Jeez, Luis. Did you buy the whole store?" This sent Luis bumbling once more, but Juli cut him off this time. "I'd be happy to teach you, we'll have to sit up here though in case I get any customers."

Luis nodded, and Juli went into the back room to grab two chairs which she placed behind the counter, next to hers. While she did this, I looked up at Luis.

"Why are we getting knitting lessons?" I asked as I tugged on the edge of his shirt.

"You seemed a bit bored at home, so I thought you needed a new hobby!" Luis smiled wide and gripped my shoulder gently before giving me a little shake.

"All of this...has been for me?" My head was light as a feather and my heart even lighter as I realized that he had given me more gifts.

Luis nodded, and about that time was when Juli returned from the back room with the chairs. We took our seats behind the counter, and Juli handed us both a pair of knitting needles and a ball of yarn each. Then, she began the slow process of teaching us how to knit. She demonstrated the 'cast on', when you make the loops you'll be using to knit, several times, and I was able to catch on pretty easily. But, Luis on the other hand was a wreck, he couldn't get his hands to cooperate with him no matter how hard he tried. Even with me also trying to explain it to him, he was lost. Eventually, he gave up and proceeded to wander around the store and tend to the flowers while Juli continued her lesson with me. An hour later, we had gotten a decent sized knitted square done. Juli then taught me how to 'cast off,' where you finish the piece and tie off your yarn. Finished, I proudly displayed my knitted square to Luis, who clapped as I held it up. Juli also joined in on the clapping and patted me on the back.

"You can make a bunch of little squares like this, and then when you have a good fifty of them, come back to me and I'll teach you how to make a small quilt out of them." Juli smiled genuinely and I felt all hesitance I had about her melt off of me. From there, Luis and I left towards home after wishing Juli a good day.

Several days passed after this, and I spent much of my time knitting. I was enthralled by my new hobby, and proceeded to thank Luis at least once a day for the gift he had given me. I had made ten squares so far, and was steadily progressing further one day when Luis walked in the house after doing some gardening. Seeing me quietly knitting, he seemed to get an idea and headed into the bedroom. He returned a bit later with book in hand and plopped down onto the couch.

"What would you think about me reading to you while you knit? That way you have something to hold your attention other than mindlessly moving the needles and yarn," Luis suggested as he held the book up with one hand.

I nodded, and he promptly opened the book and began to read. The story was about a young Hegal boy, winged demon, who was born in a city of Angels. The beginning of the book details how the boy was abandoned at the age of three by his parents, and taken in by a local orphanage. Angels notoriously hate Demons, so with the city being so full of Angels, the boy felt he had nowhere to turn. Every day he would be berated and picked on by the other children and by the residents of the city. He took solace in the small things he did have though, like his daily flights where he would soar

72

high above the city on errands for the orphanage caretakers. He also enjoyed drawing, and would draw in the dirt with a stick in the moments when the other children left him alone. That was as far as we got in the story when there came a knock on the door. Luis closed the book and set it on the couch as he stood to answer the door. Outside, there stood a Pulichi man, wolf centaur, with a saddle bag on his wolf half that he pulled a scroll from.

"A summons from Brightbane, sir. The details are enclosed," he said as he handed off the scroll to Luis and turned before sprinting off into the distance.

Luis unfurled the scroll and read it over. Then, he turned to me with a very serious expression that I hadn't seen on him before.

"I've got a quest in the capital, Cadmar. It's about a week's walk north-east from here." He walked over and set the scroll on the coffee table before kneeling in front of my chair. "My job is to watch over you, but I won't force you to come if you don't want to. So, what'll it be?"

I set my knitting down and thought for a moment as I looked at my lap. I didn't want to deal with more new people who would likely treat me as a thing not a person, but I also definitely didn't want to be away from him for who knew how long. More than anything, I didn't want to be alone. I looked back up at him and nodded. "I'll go with you."

Luis smiled and put a hand on my shoulder before standing to gather his things.

Chapter 9:

The Beginning of a Journey

After grabbing my pack, two bedrolls, my weapons, my waterskin and water stone, my armor, plenty of rations, some candles for the kid, and a few books for any down time we might have, I was ready to go. I decided walking would be best since I likely couldn't carry my armor, pack, and the kid, so we set out towards Cadmar on foot. We started our journey heading towards the village as we would get on the road to Cadmar from there. The two-hour walk passed in silence, but it was a comfortable silence and she didn't seem at all awkward or perturbed by it. When we arrived in the village, I took the chance to buy a quick snack for lunch. There was really only one meal vendor in the market, and they sold chunks of marinated steak on wooden skewers. This didn't bother me in the slightest, as I always enjoyed getting some as a little treat for myself.

Enjoying the juiciness of the meat skewer I had bought, we walked through the village and the crowd that buzzed inside of it. The thought occurred to me to stop and see Juli before leaving, but she'd probably tease me for going to see her just for that reason. *Then again, she'll probably want to know what happened to the kid and why she never showed back up to keep knitting,* I thought. My mind jumped back and forth between the options, but as Juli's shop came into view, I felt a tug on my shirt. I turned around and saw the kid standing there, looking guilty.

"Can we go see Juli before we leave?" she asked sheepishly.

I smiled wide, happy she had essentially made the decision for me, and nodded. We then headed into the flower shop where Juli was dutifully tending to the flowers, using water magic to refresh the water in the vases and water the potted flowers. She turned her head as we came in, but her hands still conducted the water around the shop as she did so.

"H-Hey, Juli," I greeted her, my knees practically clicking together with how nervous she made me.

"Well if it isn't my favorite duo. What can I do you for?"

I opened my mouth to say something, but when all I could manage was a pathetic squeak as my throat gave up on me, the kid spoke up instead.

"We're leaving to go to Cadmar. Luis has a quest," she explained.

"Oh! And you thought to come say goodbye to little old me? Well aren't you the sweetest." Juli finished using the water magic and walked over to us, wrapping one arm around each of us and giving us both a squeeze. She then giggled and turned to look at me. "Couldn't resist, eh? I guess my charms have finally won you over," she joked and elbowed me playfully as she laughed.

I bit down slightly on my tongue, unwilling to say anything, lest I accidentally confess my love for her. The kid let out a small giggle as well, and I looked down at her, my hand over my heart as I feigned betrayal. This made both of them laugh even more, and my heart fluttered with warmth as I realized that this was the first time I really saw the kid laugh. I put an arm around her shoulders and pulled her into a half hug, dragging her along before saying goodbye to Juli and heading out of the village altogether.

A couple hours into our journey, the kid didn't seem bored as she looked around at the scenery while we traveled. But I still felt the need to try to entertain her, even if only for a little bit. "You know any traveling songs, kid?" I asked as we walked down the road.

"No. I have one tune in my head that I seem to know, but I think it's a lullaby," she responded, as though questioning herself.

That honestly raised a few questions, and it occurred to me that she hadn't talked much about herself. Often just asking me questions about myself and my journeys, I knew almost nothing about her or her time with Firnyn. I knew she may have been hesitant due to the trauma he caused her, but I still felt guilty and made a mental note to ask her about it as we traveled. For now, though, I had a mission to teach her a traveling song!

"Ok, I'll teach you one then! This one is called The Road to Zaranga." I began to bellow out the song that was a staple for adventurers as it detailed the mythical road to the lost city of Zaranga. It was a fairly long song, hence why it was typically sung while traveling, and talked about the fights and perilous obstacles along said road. I finished several minutes later, and smiled wide down to her. "There! Now, I know you probably won't remember all of that, but I'll go over the chorus with you. I'll sing a line and then you sing it back to me." I sang the first line, and waited for her to reply, but I instead got an awkward silence. "Hey, what's up? Don't like to sing?"

"No, it's not that...I just...I've never sung in front of anyone before. I don't know if I'll sound good or not. What if it's screechy and hurts your ears?" She furrowed her brow and looked down to the ground as she walked onward.

"Hey, don't think like that. I probably sound like a dying walrus, but I still sing anyway. It's not about if you sound good, it's about having fun! Come on, give it a try!" I put a careful hand on her shoulder and shook her slightly to encourage her.

The kid nodded and started the line in a very quiet voice, so quiet that I could barely hear her. I shrugged, taking this to be good enough, and began to sing the next line and the next. Every time she repeated a line back to me, her voice got a little louder as she grew more comfortable until I could actually hear what she sounded like. Her voice floated out of her like golden strings of light. I stared in amazement that she had ever been worried about it at all, and then I smiled wide as she looked up at me nervously. I continued to teach her the song for the next few minutes, until she had at least the chorus down pat. We sang the song together once more through, and she seemed to genuinely enjoy herself as she even added a slight hop to her step. The next few hours passed comfortably, the kid humming the chorus every now and then as we walked. Five hours into it, we began to pass by a small grove of trees, and something caught my attention. In the center of the trees, I heard a small buzzing noise, and instinctively licked my lips in anticipation.

"Wait here, kid. I'll be right back," I said as I cracked my knuckles and walked into the tree line.

I peeked around each tree, searching the branches quickly as I walked until finally I saw it, a small beehive built in the hole of a tree. *Score!* I thought as I pulled a torch out of my bag and held it between my knees as I lit it with a flint and steel. I began blowing the smoke from the torch into the tree hole, careful not to catch the tree on fire. Once the bees had calmed down from the smoke, I doused my torch with my waterskin and carefully reached a gloved hand inside the hole. I grabbed a large piece of honeycomb that barely fit through the hole. I was about to start cutting off the wax from the honeycomb in order to release the honey into a spare bottle I had, but I heard the hive beginning to swarm. Even with my scales, the bees would be an issue if they got to the flesh beneath them or the fleshy part of my wings, so I put my pack back on my back and started booking it out of the grove. I could hear the swarm behind me getting closer, so I picked up speed.

As the kid came into view, I shouted over to her. "Time to go! Run that-a-way!" I pointed down the road wildly.

She looked at me confused for a moment until she saw the bees chasing me and spun around to run off down the road. I caught up to her easily, and we ran for a few minutes until I was sure the bees had stopped chasing us. I heaved a heavy sigh and took a few deep breaths to satisfy my aching lungs. The kid did the same, but she was much more out of breath than I, and it occurred to me that that must've been the first time she'd ever run. I patted her back softly and smiled down at her as she looked up at me tiredly.

"Let's take a break. I've got to collect my spoils of war, after all!" I said, holding up the large chunk of honeycomb that had coated my hand in a layer of honey.

She gave a tired smile and nodded, taking a seat on the hillside next to the road. I took the chance to get a glass bottle from my pack, cut off the wax caps from the honeycomb, and slowly drizzled the honey into the bottle. After I was done, I threw the honeycomb aside, and began to clean up the honey that had gotten all over my hand, by licking it up of course. I reveled in the strong sweetness of the flavor, closing my eyes as I let it fill my very being with its sweetness. I opened my eyes a few moments later, having finished cleaning off my hand, only to see the kid staring up at me and holding in a laugh.

"What? Did I get some on my face?" I began touching all over my face with my hands, searching for any traces of honey that may have been left behind.

This made the kid lose her battle with her laughter, as she giggled unabashedly. I smiled at this and elbowed her gently. This kid had really given me a soft spot for her, and as I realized this, I also made a determination; for as long as she let me, I would keep her safe and watch over her. I found myself nodding in affirmation of this thought, and the kid looked up at me curiously as I did so. I waved a hand dismissively and stood up since it seemed the kid had fully caught her breath; it was time to get back on the road.

As we walked, the kid spoke up, "So, why did you go after that hive?"

"Isn't it obvious?" I smiled mischievously. The kid shook her head, and I carefully shook the bottle of honey. "This is a *delicacy* in my book." She grinned up at me and I raised an eyebrow to her. She just kept smiling and shook her head, looking back out toward the road.

Two hours passed in our usual comfortable silence until it was sunset and time to stop for the night. We stopped by a large, lone tree on the hill and I took out my hand axe to chop off some branches to use for firewood. The thought occurred to me that the kid likely wouldn't be able to get anywhere near the campfire, so I put the axe back in its sheath on my bag. I'd have to bundle up extra tight in my bedroll to keep warm, not that it was particularly cold on summer nights, but it was better safe than sorry. We sat down in the dark next to the tree. To at least provide a little bit of light, I took one of the kid's candles out of my bag and lit it. Seeing the small candle in place of what was usually a fairly large campfire made me chuckle, and the kid looked up at me, eyebrow raised, and head tilted slightly.

"It's nothing, just strange to see a candle instead of a campfire," I explained.

"Why don't you make a campfire?" she asked, scooching a little closer.

"Oh no reason, just didn't feel like going through the trouble. It's been a long day, after all." I added emphasis to this lie by cracking my neck and knuckles loudly.

The kid stood up and held out her hand to me. "Oh, ok. Well, I'll do it then! You can just relax. Axe please!"

I chuckled awkwardly and rubbed the back of my head with one hand. "Alright, you caught me. I just didn't want you to have to sit away from the fire to stop from melting."

The kid grew red in the face, clearly still unused to having anyone care about her, and sat back down next to me. "T-Thank you," she mumbled as she fidgeted with her hands.

I nodded and gave her a slight shove. Silence set in from there, and we sat just staring at the candle in the dark until an idea occurred to me. "You know, it may not be a campfire, but that doesn't mean we can't tell campfire stories! Here, I'll go first." I began to recall the adventure I went on when I was first starting out as an adventurer. It was a harrowing tale of love and strife, and all of it ended with a satisfying conclusion. As I finished the tale, the kid clapped quietly and smiled. At this point I remembered the mental note I had made earlier and decided to act on it.
"So...You've heard plenty of my stories and adventures, but I haven't heard any of yours. I know you may not want to talk about it. Reliving that stuff is hard. But, I think it'd be good to get it off your chest. If you don't mind me being the one you tell it to, that is."

The kid's posture grew rigid, and I could tell that she didn't want to talk about it. "I don't have much to tell..." she admitted in a hushed voice.

"Well, I'll listen to anything you have to tell...You don't need to worry anymore, you know? That stuff is in the past and it's not going to hurt you ever again. I won't let it." I flexed my arm and patted my bicep with the other hand.

The kid smiled, but weakly, and looked deep into the candle's flame as she began her story. She told me about the first time she woke up, how Firnyn treated her and why, the creation of her siblings, the little bonding time she got to have with them, and then the day she was put in the closet. From there, she explained that all of her memories blended together. She said all of this like it was nothing, staying in a quiet, resigned voice, but I could tell how much it hurt her. Without thinking to ask first, I scooted over to her and pulled her into a tight hug.

"W-W-What are you doing? L-Luis? Uh-Uhm…" she sputtered, and I hugged her a little tighter, careful not to hurt her. She had been through so much, and when she finally found people to rely on, they were ripped away from her. No wonder this girl was so timid and scarred. My heart burned with sadness and rage, sadness that she had had to go through all of that and rage that Firnyn had put her through all of it.

Eventually I released her, and, leaning back, I saw her face was a deep red color and she looked dizzy. I held back a chuckle and pinched her cheek gently with my fingers. "You ok, kid?"

She nodded slowly, teetering back and forth a bit for a moment until she managed to get her bearings it seemed and looked down at her lap. "T-Thank you, Luis," she mumbled and grabbed the bedroll I had set out for her, unfurled it a pace away from me, and crawled inside. I figured I ought to do the same to be rested for tomorrow, blew out the candle, and got myself situated in my own bedroll.

The next morning, I awoke to the sound of a lute being played somewhere in the distance. It was early, the sun still rising, and the kid still lay still, fast asleep. I doubted it would be anything bad, very rarely do lutes hold ill will, but I figured I should be safe and woke the kid up with a soft shake of her shoulder. As soon as she sat up, wiping her eyes sleepily, I saw the origin of the sound, a traveling Human minstrel making his way over the hill towards us. I stood with a start as I saw him, shining my horns with my hands and straightening out my clothing to the best of my ability. I had one or two songs written about me over the years, but none that ever got overly popular. This was as good a chance as ever to see if he knew any songs about me, or even to teach him one!

81

The minstrel stopped his strumming as he got closer and swung his lute onto his back. "Hello fellow travelers! A fine day, is it not?"

I stepped forward a few paces to meet him, and held out my hand in greeting. "It is! Though the day has just started," I pointed out as he shook my hand.

"Yes, yes. It has just begun, but we must endeavor to make the day good by believing that it will be." The minstrel tapped the tip of his nose twice as he said this and grinned. "So, what brings you two to journey this way on this fine day?"

"We're headed to Cadmar. I've got a quest," I explained, trying to not sound too boastful.

The minstrel's eyes practically sparkled. "A quest in the capital, you say? You must be a fine adventurer, indeed! What is your name, good sir?"

"Luis, Luis Rockwell," I introduced myself, giving a slight bow as I did so.

The minstrel pulled the lute from his back and began to play a familiar tune. "Rockwell, slayer of Girmel the beast. He doth clothe himself in flame, and fight until Girmel was deceased!" the minstrel sang beautifully, and I nodded along as he did so.

"That would be me! You play it very well by the way," I complimented him, and put a hand on his shoulder, shaking him a bit.

He seemed flustered a bit by this and threw his lute back onto his back before righting his hat, which had tilted when I shook him. "Why thank you. That's a bit of a lousy tune, though. I could write a better one while deaf and blind!" he boasted, and I chuckled.

82

Then an idea occurred to me, and I decided I had to jump on the opportunity. "Is that so? Well, I'd love to have you join us so you can write a better one. I don't know what the exact details of the quest are, yet, but given that it's in the capital, it's likely to be a lively one!" I offered.

The minstrel bowed deeply. "I would be honored, Mr. Rockwell."

At this point, the kid had made it over to us, and she curtsied to greet the minstrel. "Hello, sir. It's nice to meet you. I overheard that you'll be traveling with us?" she asked, her voice more formal than usual.

The minstrel squeaked in surprise and covered his mouth. "Oh! Well, yes…It's nice to meet you too?" he said hesitantly as he bowed back to her.

From there we agreed to have breakfast as we walked. The kid didn't need to eat for another few days at least, but the minstrel and I ate some jerky rations that we each had packed.

"So, what's your name, minstrel?" I asked as I swallowed a bite of jerky.

"I am known simply as Melinai. A pleasure." He bowed slightly as he walked.

The following hours passed peacefully, with Melinai entertaining us with stories and songs as we journeyed through the countryside. We planned to continue journeying to get to the next village, but suddenly a summer rainstorm surprised us all. I was ready to stop and sit in a nearby tree grove to take shelter from the rain, and started moving that way when Melinai grabbed me by the arm.

"No need for that, Mr. Rockwell." Melinai then proceeded to swing his lute off his back and into his hands.

I tilted my head in confusion at first, but then instantly understood as he strummed the lute and the inside of it glowed a bight blue. The kid still looked at Melinai with confusion, but this quickly changed to amazement as the raindrops above us began to form into a floating blanket of water, protecting us from the rest of the rain. He wasn't a minstrel, but a bard, an adventurer and user of rune-carved instruments to cast magic. With our journey no longer obstructed by the rain, we continued onward, and I pat Melinai on the back in thanks as we set out once more. Before we knew it, two days passed rather quickly, with the three of us taking refuge at night in a tent that Melinai had packed and getting to know each other through talking about anything and everything during the day. By the time we made it to the next village, we had bonded quite well with Melinai.

Chapter 10:

Home is Where the Heart is?

As we arrived at the village of Swindon at sunset, Luis seemed to get uncomfortable and quiet, as he gave shorter and shorter answers to anything Melinai and I said. My confusion was made even greater, however, when we walked in on the village's main road, and everyone began to greet Luis by name. *If this is a village he's known in, why isn't he happy to be here?* I thought curiously. Luis simply gave small waves to anyone who called out to him, and he guided us over to the tavern where we would be staying the night. Walking into the small tavern, the three of us were surprised to see it was quite lively despite its size. Luis walked up to the bartender, a four-armed Ziemian woman, earth Fairy subspecies that have anywhere between four and eight arms, that greeted Luis with a wide smile.

"Luis! Welcome back! How have you been? How's the adventuring life treating you?" she greeted him warmly as she set down the glass she had been cleaning to put a hand on his shoulder.

"Hey Vel, I've been good. Can I get a room that fits three, please?" Luis said weakly, the usual sparkle in his eyes muted.

"Straight to business as usual, eh? Well, I won't press you, here's a room key. Room number four on the left. And don't stay in your room all night. Come have dinner with everyone instead, would ya?" She handed him a small bronze key and gave him a soft punch on the arm for emphasis.

85

Luis nodded and went to grab his belt pouch to pay her, but she stopped him. "You should know you stay here free! Don't even worry about it. Now come get some dinner with your friends here once you're settled," Vel insisted.

Luis nodded resignedly and led us down the hallway next to the bar to our room. It was fairly good-sized, especially for a free room, and had four cots with straw mattresses. Pushed up against the wall in front of the only window sat a small desk and chair that Melinai went straight for, plopping his pack down as he relaxed into the chair and began to tune his lute carefully. Luis set his pack down as well with a heavy thud and lay down on one of the cots. I followed Luis's example and sat down on one of the other cots, testing the softness of the mattress by bouncing up and down on it a bit. It wasn't as soft as the one back at Luis's house, but it was much better than just a bedroll on the dirt. I lay down and fall almost instantly to sleep listening to Melinai softly strum his lute.

About an hour later, well after sunset, Luis pinched my cheek softly, waking me. "Melinai and I are going to go eat and have a few drinks, do you want to stay in the room or come with us?" he asked as the light from the hallway poured into the room behind his frame.

I stood from the cot quickly, yawning as I did so, and nodded to him as I gestured for him to go ahead. He smiled weakly and walked out into the hallway with Melinai, with me following close behind. As we walked, many people in the tavern raised their drinks to Luis in greeting as he passed by. Picking the only free table, in the center of the others, Luis plopped down in a chair and motioned for us to sit with him. Melinai and I did so, and Melinai shouted over to Vel to bring them a round of drinks and two servings of food. People here still seemed to look at me strangely, but unlike the others I had encountered, they all seemed to be thrilled to see me simply because I accompanied Luis. Having the people around me talk to me brightly and warmly without hesitance

86

was incredible and warmed my heart. So, I spent the next two hours talking and laughing with the other patrons of the bar while Luis and Melinai ate and drank. When Melinai finished inhaling his meal, he stood and made his way to the small stage area in the back of the tavern where he began to play a lively tune to drum up the mood.

The next morning, Luis, Melinai, and I awoke to someone knocking on our door. Luis got up groggily, teetering as he walked over. On the other side of the door was a small Meadow Elf man who looked up at Luis apologetically. "Sorry to wake you there, Luis, but we've got a bit of a problem we were hoping you could help out with. Ya know, for old time's sake?"

"What is it, Mr. Lunorin?" Luis said tiredly, but not annoyed in the slightest.

"Well Iegark got drunk last night and fell asleep in the road in front of mine and the Iacaryn's farms, and now neither of us can get our wagons down the road. Could you take care of it please?"

Luis wiped his face with a hand and nodded before turning to Melinai and me. "Wanna come with?"

"It's too early for excitement of any kind. I'm staying here," Melinai grumbled as he turned over in his cot to face away from us.

I, on the other hand, stood up and put on my boots, ready to tag along. Luis smiled and rubbed my back as I moved past him and out the door. Once we were out of the room, Mr. Lunorin guided us out of the tavern and into the early morning sunshine where we walked through the village to what was presumably his farm. Sure enough, lying in the road and snoring loudly, was a large, Ogre man, large humanoid from the underground. He wore a tan button-down shirt with overalls and a sunhat that lay to his side. Luis sighed and mumbled something under his breath about Iegark doing this so many times in the past. Luis squatted down to try to lift the nearly ten foot, hundreds of pounds, man up out of the road. To Luis's credit, he lifted him a good foot off the ground before his arms gave out. Luis tried this for a few minutes until he finally heaved a heavy sigh and looked at Iegark with exhaustion. But then, an idea seemed to occur to him and he took a deep breath in, the glands in his neck expanding and glowing red as he did so. With a shout, he exhaled hot, but not boiling, water onto Iegark's face. His large, dark eyes shot open and he looked around as he sat up with a start.

"Oh! Luis! Welcome back! I guess I caused you some trouble again this morning, haven't I?" Iegark answered as he wiped off his face with a cloth that Mr. Lunorin provided him.

"Don't worry about it, happy I could help," Luis said as he waved a hand dismissively.

Iegark stood and gave Luis a strong handshake before apologizing to Mr. Lunorin. Luis and I turned away and headed back down the road toward the tavern.

I took the chance to ask him a question that buzzed around in my mind. "Why don't you use your ability to breathe water instead of a water stone? I'm sure it's much more convenient."

Luis shook his head. "Well, the water isn't technically my saliva since we generate the water through magic the same way water stones do, but it's been in my mouth *with* my saliva and it just feels gross to imagine using it for anything," he admitted while blushing slightly.

We continued on in silence after that, until an old Human woman waved us over. Luis seemed to grow stiff and awkward once more as we approached her.

"Luis! Hello again, dear." She grabbed Luis's hand and held it in both of hers. "You should come visit more often, you know."

"I know…I'm sorry Jen," he replied guiltily.

"Oh it's alright, I know it can be hard for you. But don't forget that your family is here for you!" She patted his hand softly as she said this and then released it. "Well, I won't keep you, but do go say 'hi' to Dad, would you? He worries about you, you know."

Luis swallowed hard and simply nodded waving to the woman as she began walking off in the opposite direction.

Luis then looked to me, "Do you…Do you mind if we run an errand?"

I shook my head no, and Luis nodded, starting to walk down a side road between farms. Following after him was pretty easy, as he went slower than normal, as though dreading something. "Luis? Do you mind if I ask who that was?" I asked meekly, my heart beating loudly in my ears.

Luis kept his eyes on the road and stayed silent for a few moments before finally answering. "That was my younger sister, Jen."

I was completely lost by this point. "But, that was an old woman. A *Human* woman!"

"Yeah…She was born thirty years after me. My mom was a Human," Luis said, and winced as the word 'mom' left his mouth. When two different races intermingled, it was not unheard of to have some children of one race and others of another, but more commonly all children would be of one of the parents' races. In extremely rare circumstances, it would lead to a mixing of the races, creating a Halfbreed.

From there Luis seemed to want to stay silent, so I walked with him quietly, not wanting to pressure him. After a few minutes, we arrived at a farmhouse on a fairly large farm, and Luis stopped a few paces away from the porch, hesitantly. Not knowing what to say, I simply took Luis's hand in mine and smiled up at him. This seemed to shake him from the shackles in his mind and he gave my hand a squeeze before walking up the steps to the front door. He let go of my hand as he knocked. A few moments passed until finally, an Older Wynorm man opened the door. The man smiled wide, a smile that it occurred to me looked starkly similar to Luis's.

"Son! Welcome home!" He pulled a stoic Luis into a tight hug. "Oh, and you brought a…friend? Whatever, just come in, come in. I'll make you some tea."

Luis's dad moved into the house, leaving the door open as a way of insisting that Luis follow him. Luis sighed, his breath tight and upset, but moved inside nonetheless. Inside, it was decorated with many floral patterns as well as potted flowers hanging from chain holders that hung from the ceiling in every windowsill. As Luis walked inside, he went over to the pots and inspected the leaves of each one before calling over to his dad who was in the kitchen. "You really should water these a little less, the roots are going to mold and die."

"Oh, I know, but your mother was always so much better with flowers than I was. You can't expect me to do better than her or your standards!" His dad called back over to him.

Luis and I sat down on the couch, and Luis's dad returned a few minutes later with two teacups and a teapot. He then poured some tea into each of the cups and handed one to Luis, before taking the second for himself.

"I hope you don't mind, I figured you didn't drink tea," he said to me, and I smiled politely, shaking my head.

Luis took a sip of his tea, and then took a deep breath as though preparing himself for something. "I saw Jen. She seems well," Luis said with bated breath. The smile Luis's father wore slipped off his face suddenly into a scowl. "Yep, that's what I thought." Luis stood with a start, slamming the teacup onto the coffee table with a loud thud that threatened to break the cup entirely. "Won't even care about your own daughter as she grows old. She's not going to be around forever you know, she's going to join mom on that hill, and you'll have no one left that cares about your sorry ass." Luis's voice was hard and tight as he spoke, as though trying to hold back the emotions that flooded inside of him.

Luis's dad looked up at him with a pitiful expression. "I'll have you though! Won't I? So, I don't need *that creature* in our lives."

Luis winced as his father called his sister a creature, and then shook his head, "You haven't had me for a long time, Dad. And until you can accept Jen, you won't have me ever again."

Luis motioned for me to follow him, and we left out the back door towards the farm fields. Luis walked in a silent rage that I dared not interrupt. We walked through two fields before we came to a grassy hill where there sat a very large, old oak tree. Next to the tree sat a small headstone, and suddenly I understood why we were here. Luis knelt down next to the headstone and hung his head as he seemed to offer a prayer to the Gods. He stayed like that for several moments, and I stood a few paces away, not wanting to intrude into the sacred moment he was having with his mother's memory. Eventually, he swiped at some tears that threatened to fall, and stood, walking back over to me. I thought that we would go back to the tavern at this point, but I saw Luis sit down at the base of the tree, so I quickly joined him. He looked out over the farm sternly for a few minutes until he finally spoke.

"Mom was a Human that was born and raised on this farm along with several generations of her family before her. She was the sweetest lady you'd ever meet, always helping anyone who needed it. She's the reason I became an adventurer. She passed away about sixty years ago, when I was just a kid. She died giving birth to Jen.

And it's a sad situation, losing your Mom and gaining a sister all in the same day. But, I loved Jen, and I wasn't about to let Mom's sacrifice be in vain. So, I treated her like a princess, there wasn't anything I wouldn't do for that kid. But, Dad...Dad was broken. He had lost the love of his life and ended up with a Human child that he had no idea how to raise on his own. So, instead of trying to put himself together at least enough to take care of us, he completely ignored that Jen existed, treating her as an abomination. And would you believe it, all these years later and she still lives in this miserable little village, and checks on Dad every day no matter how horrible he treats her. That's why I don't come back here very often. Just the memories and the whole situation, I hate it. It *hurts*...I think the thing that makes it the worst is knowing how hurt Mom would be to know how we all ended up, a broken family." At this point, tears freely flowed down Luis's cheeks, and without thinking, I pulled him into a hug. I was at least a good foot and a half shorter than him, so the hug was a little awkward, but he chuckled and hugged me tightly back. "Thanks, kid."

After I released him, we sat under that tree for about five minutes, just staring out at the farmland. I wanted to say something, to reassure him. To fix his predicament. But, I also knew that it wasn't my place to do so, and that I might just offend him if I did say anything. So, I waited patiently in silence until Luis stood up and offered me his hand. I took it and he pulled me to my feet with one swift motion. From there, we walked back through the farmland, past the farmhouse and onto the road towards the tavern. Once we got to the tavern, I went to the room to wake up Melinai, and Luis ordered a plate and drinks for the both of them. Melinai was awake when I got to the room, so all I had to do was invite him out to have breakfast with us. Melinai agreed, and while he and Luis ate their breakfast of bread and porridge with some wine to drink, I cracked into one of my candles that Luis had packed. We had opted to bring only plain candles, as we had more of those, and to my surprise I found myself missing the flavor of the scented ones.

Eating in front of people made me a bit self-conscious since I noticed they all winced whenever I bit into the candle. But I could ignore my feelings about eating as I was paying more attention to Luis, who still seemed down about what had happened. I did my best to try to get him to tell me a story or encourage him to sing along with Melinai, but nothing worked. My heart sunk deep into the depths of my stomach as I realized there was nothing I could do to help him. With this in mind, I resigned to simply supporting him through gentle nudges and pats on the back, hoping that would ease his pain, even if only a little bit. We all packed up an hour later and got back on the road to Cadmar. With four more days of journeying ahead of us, we set out as quickly as we could.

The first day after leaving Swindon was quiet. Luis was still lost in his mind, likely still upset about his father and sister, and Melinai caught onto this heavy feeling, refusing to play his lute for the entire day. The second day, on the other hand, was completely different. Luis woke Melinai and me up at the crack of dawn with a wide smile on his face and a skip in his step. I was about to ask what had changed, but seemingly reading my mind Melinai shook his head at me and held up a finger to his mouth in a 'hush' motion. Luis didn't catch sight of this as he focused on making Melinai and himself breakfast from a rather large rabbit he had caught. The rest of the day, Luis was overly chipper, and it occurred to me that he was likely forcing himself to move on for our sakes. Not wanting his efforts to be wasted, I simply went along with his 'happiness'. The next two days were much the same as the one before it, only Luis was much more himself, he had a natural cheer rather than forced.

Chapter 11:

Monster

Cadmar appeared on the horizon halfway through the day, and it was as formidable a sight as I remembered it. The capital of Aethos had always amazed and enchanted me, and seeing it again made me feel a sense of peace and homeliness. Arriving at the city gates deepened that feeling as I saw some familiar faces among the guards there.

"Uthril! Han! How have you guys been?" I had met these two when I first came to Cadmar five years ago to join the guild here.

"Luis, ya bastard! Welcome back to the capital!" Uthril, a stout Dwarvish man, chuckled as he ran up to meet us.

"Greetings, Luis. It is good to see you are well," said Han, a fox Piztia, demons with animal ears and tails, as he bowed slightly.

I laughed heartily and wrapped an arm around each of them, pulling them into a tight hug. Uthril patted my back and chuckled along as well, while Han squirmed uncomfortably.

"I have missed you as well, dear friend, but please release me." Han said with a tight voice; he was never much of one for displays of affection.

I chuckled again and released both of them before turning to gesture to the kid and Melinai. "These are my traveling companions. The kid I'm watching over as part of a different quest than the one I'm here for, and the bard, Melinai, here is going to write a song about me!"

"Another song for this old codger? I don't know, perhaps another song will make his ego even bigger than it already is!" Uthril joked and elbowed me.

"Oh hush, you! And you're older than me, *you* old codger!" I elbowed him back a little too hard and knocked him back a few steps.

This made everyone laugh, and after our laughter had settled, I patted Uthril and Han on the shoulders "Well, boys. I'm off to the tavern. It's going to be sunset soon, and we've been traveling all day. I'll be at our usual place when you get off work tonight though!"

They both waved us off happily with a promise to meet up for drinks later that night, and the kid, Melinai, and I went through the city gates and onto the main road. As usual the road was packed with people, making the crowds of Tithridge look absolutely pitiful. The wide cobblestone streets led through the housing district, straight to the heart of the city where the market district lay nestled between the other housing areas. Here is where I led my companions, since in the heart of the market was a massive tavern, the Dry Grotto; the best place in town to get lodging, food, and drinks. As we walked in the door, I immediately looked to the bar. Just as I expected, Clark, one of the evening bartenders, was busy at work serving drinks and talking to patrons of the tavern. I walked up and slid my way between the gaps in the stools and knocked on the bar with one hand. As soon as Clark saw me, his face lit up and he quickly finished up his conversation. As he was moving over to me, I looked behind me to check on the kid and Melinai, and was happy to see that Melinai was ushering the kid over to a table. Melinai caught my gaze with his and shouted out to grab him and myself some food and drinks.

"Luis! It's good to see you! What's it been? Three years? Four?" He held back a laugh, covering his mouth with one hand as he leaned on the bar with the other.

"It's been three *months*, Clark. And how have you been, you sssnake?" I teased him, drawing out the 's' since he was in fact a Lamia, half human-half snake.

"Ah it's been the usual, livin' the dream, ya know?" he said with complete honesty, as it was his dream to be a bartender.

Five years ago, when I first came to Cadmar, I met him destitute in an alley. I didn't have much money at the time, so I just sat and talked with him for a bit that day. After that it became a habit, I would sit with him every morning. Things changed, though, when I finished my training at the guild and I had to leave Cadmar to go on adventures with my new party. Since the guild provided me with gear and food for the journey, I decided to spend my last gold piece to get Clark cleaned up nice, fed, and set up with an interview at the tavern. I departed before learning what came of the interview, but I hoped beyond hope that he would get the job. Now I visited him every time I came back into the city for the past four and a half years, often choosing to pay to stay in the tavern rather than stay free at the guild hall so I could spend more time with him. He was a great friend.

"Good to hear! Keep up the good work! Oh, and two mugs of ale and two servings of dinner for our table over there, please." I turned to walk away, but he stopped me, reaching out a hand. I raised an eyebrow at him as I turned back to face him.

He leaned across the bar toward me and whispered, "I saw your old party today, and uh, let's just say they aren't doing very well. If you happen to run into them, do keep an eye out. You know how they can be."

I nodded and patted him on the shoulder in thanks before turning away and heading back to the table. Clark nodded, winked, and went off to prepare the drinks and food. A few moments later, as I was sitting with the kid and Melinai, a barmaid brought round our order. I paid and tipped her, and she smiled wide before heading off to the other tables. Melinai and I ate quickly, tired from the long day of journeying, and needing some sustenance to make up for it. The kid sat quietly, taking in everything around her, and I noticed as I finished eating that she was getting more than a few uncomfortable stares.

I leaned over and pinched her arm gently and whispered in her ear, "Remember what I said, yeah? You're freaking *fantastic*. Don't let people who don't understand that get you down."

I leaned back away from her to see her face, and she smiled slightly, nodding. She was still clearly uncomfortable by everyone looking at her like that, but at least I got her to smile. Then an idea occurred to me and I leaned over to whisper to Melinai, "Give us a grand performance, would you?"

"Why of course, Mr. Rockwell!" Melinai grinned and went over to the stage, a much larger one than back in Swindon.

Melinai began to play a soft tune, slowly casting his magic as he did so. Above everyone's heads appeared a large swan made of light which proceeded to fly and spin and dance along to the song. Every eye in the room gravitated to the illusion, and watched the swan and listened to the gentle tune. Then the pace of the song picked up, the swan stopped dancing and spinning, and flew in the air as the buildup in the music began. As the actual, lively tune started playing and Melinai began singing, the swan burst into a thousand tiny lights that floated in the air and bobbed up and down to the beat. The tavern burst into an uproar at this, amazed by the spectacle and singing along with Melinai to the familiar tavern song, *Johnny Doth he Drink too Much*. After the song finished, the cheers demanded an encore and Melinai happily obliged. As he played, the tavern doors opened, and a group of off-duty guards came in, including Uthril and Han. I waved them over, and they happily joined us, pulling up chairs so that they could fit around the smaller table.

"Time to get the party started!" Uthril cracked his knuckles as he sat down.

"Though it would appear, Uthril, that the party has already begun," teased Han.

"Oh, whatever! No party even compares to the one we are about to start! The famous trio!" Uthril declared and elbowed both Han and me.

"Go ahead and order us a round of drinks, won't you, Uthril?" Han asked, and Uthril immediately shouted out to get a barmaid's attention. As soon as Uthril had finished ordering drinks and the barmaid ran off to go get them, Han looked to me with a more serious expression. "Well, are you going to properly introduce us to the young lady? Oh, and an explanation is in order as to what this 'quest' is that entails you watching over her. It better not be that you have taken a liking to her and are dragging her along. Besides, I thought you liked Ju-" Han said, but I quickly cut him off, leaning over the table to cover his mouth with my hand.

"Shut. It." I chuckled awkwardly and sat back down before clearing my throat and pulling at the neckline of my shirt. "Well, it's a quest from the URA," I said in a quiet tone so as not to drum up too much excitement.

Both of them practically screamed, "THE URA?!"

"Shhhh!" I pulled both of them closer to me and continuing in a hushed tone, I explained the situation at length; killing Firnyn, the kid and my meeting, and the URA meeting where I volunteered to look after her for the year. "Oh and yeah, kid, this is Uthril and Han. Guys, this is kid."

"Surely you don't just call her 'kid'? What's her real name?" Han asked, squinting at me in disbelief.

I was about to answer, but the kid answered for me. "I don't have a name," she muttered.

Uthril and Han looked at her in surprise, and then back to me with confusion. "Really?" said Uthril. The kid and I both nodded.

They looked completely flabbergasted, and honestly, I understood. I imagined that I would be in just as much disbelief about everything if I hadn't been there myself. Just then, the barmaid returned with our drinks which Uthril paid for with the promise that I'd get the next round.

"So, lassie, what's it like living with the old man, here?" Uthril asked the kid, and I laughed, rolling my eyes.

The kid looked down at her lap and said honestly, "Luis is very nice to me. Even when I feel like I don't deserve it, he lets me live with him and buys me gifts. I'm very thankful for him."

Uthril and Han both pouted their lips and squinted their eyes at me, implying that I was into the kid. I pointed a finger and dragged it quickly across my neck, telling them to cut it out. The kid's cheeks reddened again and I found myself smiling earnestly at her as she so easily melted my heart with just a stare. The guys saw this and immediately began whooping and hollering, pushing me back and forth in my seat. This loudness got more than a few eyes on us, and I desperately tried to shut them up. For the next three hours we sat talking and jesting and singing to the music Melinai played while the kid sat quietly smiling at all of us. I checked in with her a few times to make sure she wasn't bored or overwhelmed, but every time she assured me that she was fine.

The next day, after spending an hour throwing my guts up and fighting the hang over, I finally thought to go get a hangover cure from the bartender. The morning bartender, a Satyr woman that I didn't recognize, quickly sold me the potion. I chugged down the magic elixir, and instantly my head began to clear as the migraine faded away. Those potions were always on the expensive side, but I didn't mind the extra expense, knowing that I couldn't and shouldn't show up to the guild hall with a hangover. Mika would never let me hear the end of it if I did. Hangover now cured, I went to the room to get Melinai and the kid. The kid wouldn't be going with me on the quest, but I planned to leave her at the guild hall so they could watch over her. Melinai on the other hand was going to tag along so he could write a song about the epic quest this was bound to be. He would also offer some support magic just in case things got dicey.

The three of us cleaned up and left the tavern with haste. We walked through the early morning crowd, down the street a few hundred feet to Cadmar's guildhall, Brightbane. With a building much larger than anything else around it, including even the tavern, and a large training ground out the back, it was a formidable sight no matter how many times I saw it. The yellow banners waved in the breeze from the top of the building, depicting a bleeding heart with a sword stabbed into its side and a glowing crown floating over it. The guild crest was a symbol that, when I first joined, I didn't understand or like, but now it was a part of me, a symbol of pride and honor in protecting and helping those around us. I took a deep breath and walked in. Instantly I was bombarded by Mika, a white fox Tsusei, animalistic humanoid, as she questioned where I had been, why it had taken me so long to get there, and why I had two people following me.

"Good to see you too, Boss." I resisted the urge to chuckle as I said it, and instead likely sounded like I was irritated.

"Oh, there's no time for pleasantries! Come with me!" She whipped around and led us through the guildhall to a back hallway that led to her office.

Inside, was a gigantic room filled with thick books and scrolls that recorded the guild's day to day business. Mika sat down heavily in her large leather chair behind her desk and motioned for us to sit. As I sat my eyes darted around the place, looking for Mika's familiar, Nomad, which always seemed to pop up at random times to try to scare anyone in the office.

101

"Now, I didn't detail much in the message scroll, but the situation is somewhat dire. You see, the crazy old wizard Xudias died last month and left a mess that we unfortunately have to clean up. It would appear that his familiar, a magical animal of metal and flesh that he either created or summoned through the help of a god or something equally as powerful, is still in the house and won't let anyone come inside without killing them. We've lost a good fifteen guards and three newbie parties to this thing, and it hordes their bodies so we can't even give our people proper burials." Mika's voice was tight with rage as she dug her claws into the wood of her desk.

I listened tensely, readying myself for the task before me, and then cleared my throat as Mika signaled that I could go ahead and speak. "Why haven't you sent in Traz, or Ciedel's Knights, or even the Raven Legion?"

"They are all at least a month's journey away, and we don't have a month. We need to get into that house before something is accidentally released. Who knows what other crazy things he has just sitting in there? We can't risk them getting into the wrong hands." She sighed and released her grip on the desk. "Listen, this is probably a job for someone more skilled than you, your fears are founded. But you're all we've got right now. Go bring those people home. They deserve a proper resting place."

I looked at her incredulously, as telling me that I probably wouldn't succeed wasn't exactly a confidence boost.

Seeing the look on my face, she sighed once more. "I suppose I can send Nomad along with you."

I tried not to show my immediate displeasure to this idea and was about to ask where Nomad was when I felt a trickle of water hit my neck and go down my back. I stood from my seat and turned around as I looked up. In the darkness of the rafters, I caught sight of the light reflecting off of two large green eyes. The instant that we locked eyes, the shape moved rapidly, flapping its

102

large silver dragon wings until the beast landed on the desk in front of Mika, sending papers flying everywhere. It was a magical dire wolf, six feet tall, its pure white fur sprinkled with blue scales, and a large pair of dragon wings on its back. I held in a sigh and gritted my teeth as I smiled.

"Looks like we'll be working together for a little while, buddy," I said stiffly, attempting unsuccessfully to sound excited.

Nomad scoffed and turned to look down at Mika. *Yeah, I'm not exactly thrilled either,* I thought. They seemed to have some kind of conversation quietly, and as they did, I looked over to Melinai and the kid. Melinai was humming to himself as he fidgeted with his ring. The kid, on the other hand, was captivated by Nomad. She looked like she desperately wanted to pet him or speak to him, I couldn't tell which. Mika and Nomad finished their whispers and Nomad jumped down from the desk and stood in front of me. I was a little over seven feet tall, but having a magical dire wolf that's almost as tall as me was definitely a little intimidating. He looked like he was about to scoff at me once more, but instead he opened his mouth and exhaled a blast of water into my face. Nomad was able to create water just like me, though he couldn't heat his. I had half a mind to do it right back to him, but I stopped myself as Nomad simply nodded and went over to sit by the kid and Melinai.

"So, who are your companions?" Mika asked.

"This is the kid, and Melinai the bard. And about that, I was wondering if you could watch over her for a bit while I'm on the quest. It's a part of another quest I have," I explained, smiling meekly in hopes she wouldn't flat out deny me.

"Yeah, I can watch over her, just do your best to take care of the monster quickly," Mika said resignedly.

I nodded and we all got up to leave. Back in the main hall of the guild, I knelt down to talk to the kid. "Hey, listen. I'll be right back, and Mika is great, so you'll be safe with her."

The kid nodded, but looked like she had something she wanted to say. I raised an eyebrow at her, and she sputtered out a reply, "I know you're probably going to have to kill it, but just because it was made doesn't make it a monster, right?" She looked up at me with wide, worried eyes.

"Of course not! Of course not, kid. That is never what that means. She probably called it a monster because it's killed so many people. That's all," I explained and then pinched her cheek gently before winking and turning to leave.

Chapter 12:

No Place to Hide

Luis, Melinai, and Nomad left the guildhall together to head towards the quest. I, on the other hand, settled into a large chair in the front lounge. I watched Mika move dexterously around the room, darting between people and the bar and the quest board. Occasionally, she'd have to go do paperwork in her office and she'd have me go with her. I insisted that I wouldn't try to leave, but she had none of that and insisted on keeping an eye on me. I stayed in the guildhall like that for several hours, patiently waiting for Luis and Melinai to return victorious. But as the daylight grew scarce, my heart began to race as my palms became sweaty and uncomfortable. *What if something's gone wrong?* I thought, followed by a series of 'what if's and hypotheticals, all that ended in Luis being in trouble somewhere. Maybe he needed *my* help. As this thought occurred to me, I didn't even stop to think how I would possibly help him, when Mika went to the bar to talk to someone, I darted from the lounge chair and out the door. I sprinted as fast as I could down the street, dodging and weaving between people. I swore I could hear Mika somewhere behind me, threatening to take me back there, back to where I couldn't help Luis.

So, I ran and ran, stopping only once my lungs felt like they were going to explode. I dropped to my knees as I stopped in the middle of the road. I looked around while I caught my breath, taking in my surroundings, only to find I had no idea where I was. The crowd thinned out here, and there were very few people passing me by. It looked like I was in a residential area, though I didn't recognize it as the one we had walked through to get to the tavern. I stood up and dusted off my dress with the thought that I needed to find Luis, being lost could wait until I knew he was safe. I searched around through the streets, looking down every alleyway and turning down whatever side street I thought looked like a good place to turn. After an hour of this, with me being no closer to finding Luis than I was an hour before, my head began to spin. *Where am I? Where is Luis? What am I going to do?*

Suddenly, I remembered that Mika had given us the name of the wizard whose house Luis and Melinai went to. Overjoyed that I could possibly find Luis, I ran up to the first people I saw to ask for directions. It was a group of three men, all middle aged, one Angel, one Earth Elemental, and one High Elf. They looked more than a little intoxicated and smiled down at me devilishly. My stomach dropped as I realized that I may have chosen the wrong people to approach. But it was too late for as I took a step back, the one in the center, the Angel, snatched my wrist and held my arm up in the air, almost lifting me off the ground as well.

"Tch, for a tiny thing, you sure weigh a lot." The Angel looked to his sides where the other two had moved in to surround me.

"Well, it's made of candle wax. Stuff's heavy, isn't it?" responded the Earth Elemental.

The Angel shrugged and leaned in to look at my face. "So, what are we gonna do with it? It's not bad looking, and it feels like real skin, just a little waxy!"

The other two reached out to touch me, one touching my other arm, while the other pinched my face. I squeezed my eyes shut tight, dreading what would happen and desperately hoping beyond hope that Luis would come to save me.

"It looks scared, Gil. Is that even possible?" said the High Elf, I assumed since it was a different voice than the other two.

"Of course not! Don't be stupid, Alai. Golems don't have feelings, they're not *people*." The Angel replied and I heard him hit the High Elf. But then as I opened my eyes, the Angel leaned in to look at me again. "Huh, you're right, it does look scared, maybe its master made it seem that way. Smart man, I like his taste."

I opened my mouth to say something, anything, or even scream, but nothing came out, and the Angel took the chance of my mouth being open to stick his fingers in my mouth.

"Ha! No way! It has saliva too! Oh, this is gonna be fun." The Angel gave a dastardly chuckle and began talking and jesting about what they were going to do with me.

I looked around, and saw some people passing by, but they looked away from us, refusing to acknowledge my existence, my pain. With nowhere to go, and no one to save me, I at first just hung there limply, steeling myself for what was about to happen. But then I saw Luis in my head. He was in his garden, telling me that I was 'freaking fantastic.' If I let them do this, I realized in that moment that I'd never be able to look Luis in the eyes again; out of fear, out of shame. I let this feeling boil inside of me until it reached its breaking point.

The High Elf reached out to touch my chest, and in that moment, I closed my eyes and finally managed to get my voice to work. "No!" was what I screamed, my voice erupting from me as I felt the warmth of my feelings fill my entire body. But it wasn't my feelings, for when I opened my eyes, I found that I was enveloped in flames. The three men had dropped me and began to run, unwilling to confront whatever had just happened. I stood there, my mind racing between options for several minutes, until finally I opted to just sit in the middle of the road where I wouldn't burn down anything. I sighed and tried to relax, ready to wait out the flames, but just as I breathed out, they began to dissipate. Almost as quickly as they had appeared, the flames vanished, and surprisingly left no damage to my body behind. I inspected myself carefully, waiting to find a hole or a burn mark, anything, but there wasn't any. I looked around, there were one or two people that stared at me fearfully, keeping their distance. I bit my lip and furrowed my brow, not knowing where to go, how to find Luis, how to be found.

I refused to give up or stay put in case the men returned, so I stood and began to walk. Most of the houses here already had their lights out; no safe haven available. My mind felt like it was beginning to fill with tar; a thick, burning ick that clouded my mind. But then I noticed a building with lights on at the end of the side road I was on. It was a fairly large building made of clean-cut stone and marble with large stained glass windows that seemed to just be a random array of colors rather than an image or pattern. I quickly headed up to the door, and opened one of the heavy wooden doors carefully. Inside, there was a large space filled with pews, a stage at the very back to which all the pews faced and an altar sat, and a man wearing light blue robes kneeling in one of the pews near the altar. *This must be a temple,* it occurred to me, and I suddenly felt a sense of relief as I had always heard of temples giving sanctuary to those in need.

I walked in, letting the door close naturally behind me with a small squeak, and went to sit in one of the pews. I sat fairly close to the door, and decided to offer a prayer to the Gods. I had never been particularly religious, but I knew of religion and that on occasion Gods could perform miracles. It was safe to say that I was at a point where I needed a miracle, so I figured I'd give a shot in the dark. I didn't know which God this temple was dedicated to, but I prayed anyway, kneeling just like the man in the pew by the altar. I folded my hands and pressed them to my forehead as I closed my eyes. *Please let me find Luis,* I repeated in prayer over and over again in my head. I was interrupted soon, though, as the man from the front pews tapped me on the shoulder. I looked up at him, confused as to what he wanted, but he stared at me with a scowl.

"I don't know what your master told you, but we do not allow golems to offer prayers in the place of their masters. Return

108

to your master, creature, you are not welcome here." The Dark Elf man said with a thick accent that I didn't recognize.

I was shocked, I had always known temples to be a place of sanctuary to all in need, and yet I was getting kicked out. "I-I am not a Golem, sir priest," I stuttered in reply.

The man, clearly not expecting me to be able to speak, screamed and jumped backwards a good few feet. He looked me up and down fearfully. "The Gods have clearly sent a dastardly creature like you to punish us. Out! Out with you, devil beast!" the priest yelled as he pointed at me.

Tears perched in my eyes, and not knowing where to go, I stood and began to walk slowly, resignedly towards the door. I stopped, though, as I heard a voice call out. "Wait!" said the voice.

I turned to see who it was and saw that it was another priest. This one was a Highland Orc and wore more decorative robes than the one that had yelled at me, though. I looked at the new priest expectantly, hoping he wasn't going to kick me out as well.

"I'm terribly sorry, young lady. My priest is clearly devoid of manners," the Highland Orc said while shooting a glare in the other priest's direction. "My name is Margub, and I am the High Priest of this temple, the temple of Qilios. You are most welcome to find refuge here." Margub bowed his head and then smiled at me.

I found relief from my worries once more, as I took his welcome to be the truth. "Thank you, sir. May I ask, what is your God the God of? I've never heard of them before."

"Of course, child! Qilios is the God of Knowledge. We that follow him believe in bettering our minds through rigorous studies in order to grow closer to him, to be worthy of him. This is his symbol, the eye represents his endless knowledge, the book is his followers, and the candle is the light in the dark that knowledge provides us," he explained slowly, keeping eye contact with me to ensure that I was understanding what he was saying. I nodded in interest. "Why don't we continue this talk in the library?" he suggested and gestured to the door he had come through off to the left of the altar.

I smiled and agreed, heading over to the door. I heard Margub and the other priest whispering to each other, and it sounded like Margub was scolding the other priest. I sighed in relief, I was safe here, I could tell. Once I stepped through the door, I was greeted by the sight of a large library. It was bigger than the temple itself and had hundreds of shelves of books on three different floors. The floor I walked out onto from the door appeared to be the second floor, and I made my way down the steps near the center of the room to go down to what appeared to be a lounge area for reading. I relaxed into one of the couches and let my head lay against the back of the couch for a moment until I heard Margub sit in a chair across from the couch.

"So, my child. Do you mind if I ask why you're here?" Margub folded his hands and rested his elbows on his knees as he leaned towards me a bit.

I began the story of today slowly, hesitantly, but the more I talked and saw how he listened without judgment, the more comfortable I became. I finished my story a few minutes later with me arriving at the temple since I had nowhere to go.

"Well, I'm sorry to hear that. I'm sure your friend is just fine, I can feel it." Margub leaned forward and gently took my hand to squeeze it for emphasis and reassurance.

I found myself tear up in sheer relief. There was something about this priest that made me feel like I could trust him, that I could rely on him.

"So, speaking of your friend, is he the one that made you, if I may ask?" he asked softly and hesitantly.

I shook my head, and then gave him a shortened version of the story of my life so far. Since having told Luis the story, I found

110

it easier to talk about the second time around. Margub listened intently and with concern, and when I had finished my tale, he smiled worriedly. "I'm so sorry all of that happened to you, my child. But, I am glad that you found someone to rely on. The way you talk about him, though, it sounds like you revere him quite a bit."

"Of course, I do! He saved me. I can never repay that debt nor the kindness he has shown me," I insisted.

"I see, but is that all it is? Appreciation for what he's done for you?" Margub asked leadingly.

"Yes…I think? What else is there?" I asked, confused.

"Well, let me ask you this. How do you feel about Luis?"

I hung my head as I thought. In my mind, an image of Luis formed, and instantly I felt my heart rate quicken and my stomach felt like it was ready to fly out of me. "I mean, he makes me feel dizzy and wonderful and sick all at the same time."

Margub smiled knowingly and asked another leading question, "So how do you view him then? A savior? A parental figure? A friend? Something…more?"

I pondered this question at length until it finally occurred to me what he meant. I blushed and put my hand up to my face in surprise at this revelation. I had been so blind to it, I guess I just needed someone to give me a push in the right direction. My mind swirled with the realization, but I snapped out of it as a thought occurred to me. "Why do you ask all of this stuff by the way? You're a priest, not a counselor," I asked skeptically.

Margub chuckled, "People come here to seek knowledge and comfort, whether that be comfort in knowing their prayers are heard or comfort knowing that we as priests are here to be relied on. I have many parishioners that I lend an ear and advice to, even if it's not about religion or my studies. I believe that being a priest of a temple means supporting the people who worship here through anything and everything." I found myself smiling at this idea and the sentiment behind it. Seeing my smile, Margub continued. "But to answer your question more directly, I seek to guide you, so that you feel a little less lost than you felt before, even if you are in fact still lost. I believe Qilios guides my hand in times like these to ask the right questions."

I nodded, and he smiled as he stood, reaching out a hand towards me. I took it and he helped me stand. We then walked around the library slowly as we talked.

"So, my child. If you feel this way for him, do you think it is because he is your savior and nice to you, or is it because of who he is on the inside?" Margub asked as he brushed his fingertips gently against the bindings of the books while he walked.

"I-I think it's both. Is it ok for it to be both?" I looked up at him with a pit in my stomach.

"That is for you to decide, not me. But, do think on it and let me know what you decide."

I nodded and bit my lip in thought as we made one full lap around the library before I reached a conclusion. "I think it's ok. He hasn't used his position as my savior to demand anything of me, and he seems to genuinely care about me," I mumbled.

"I see. But do you believe it would be best for you to get more attached to him? Wynorms do live quite a long time, but they do die. You mentioned that you don't age, so you will likely outlive him by quite a bit," he said gently, and though it was clear he was trying to not upset me, I found myself crying at the thought.

"I don't know…" I whimpered.

"Well let me instead ask you this, you are a person, are you not?"

I nodded silently

"Then you are worthy and deserving of happiness, just as much as any other person. So I'll ask again, would it be for the best?" he asked, looking up at the ceiling as we walked.

I thought for a moment, and then wiped my tears as I spoke. "Yes, it'd be for the best. Even if I outlive him, having that happiness for as long as I can have it would make everything else worth it."

Margub nodded, satisfied. "Good. With that in mind, I say you go for it! He clearly cares about you. Sparking that into something more shouldn't be too hard."

I nodded, blushing. I was about to thank him, but suddenly, the door to the temple flew open and Luis called out my name.

Chapter 13:

A Heart of Metal and Flesh

After leaving the kid with Mika, I went with Melinai and Nomad to the far east side of town. As we got closer to the large manor that Xudias owned during his time alive, we found that the entire block of the street was shut down, barricaded, and guarded. The guards let us pass when they recognized Mika's familiar, and we headed over to a large tent that sat a few hundred feet away from the front door of the manor. I lifted the tent flap, letting Melinai and Nomad go in first. Inside they had set up a war table with a map of the manor and several X's in red. Around this table were four regular guards and one guard captain, though it should be noted he was the captain of this situation, not of the city. The city's guard captain was a very amicable man that always welcomed me into the city and helped me on quests where he could. This captain, on the other hand, looked stoic and grizzled, and I had a sinking feeling he wasn't going to like me very much.

"Oh, you're from the guild, yeah? Come take a look," said the captain, an Oni, medium-sized humanoids from the underground, that had a special helmet to allow for his five large horns to poke through.

We obediently approached the table, Melinai and I across from the captain, and Nomad to the side on a cushion that happened to be there, looking disapprovingly at all of us. The captain shot a worried glance at Nomad, and I instantly knew why, Nomad had a glint of deviousness in his eye. I looked at the manor map more closely, and could tell that the x's were where they presumed fallen 'soldiers' lay dead inside the manor. I looked up at the captain and pointed to the map.

"Are there-" I got cut off by Nomad blasting a stream of water in my face as soon as I opened my mouth.

"Oh, Nomad, friend perhaps-" Melinai started nervously only to be blasted in the face as well, only this one set him off-balance as he fell to the floor.

"Now, listen here dog-" The captain was cut off as Nomad blasted him in the face too.

Nomad lifted his head in victory, an evil look in his eyes. I opened my mouth to speak, and noticed Nomad begin to summon some water. A stalemate ensued for a minute until finally the captain broke the silence.

"Don't make me get Mika!" the captain warned.

As soon as he heard Mika's name, his happiness slipped off into a deep furrowed brow and frown. He then scoffed at the captain, and laid down on the cushion, defeated, at least for now.

I wiped the water off my face with one hand and cleared my throat. "Now, as I was saying, are there any other entrances that we can approach this from that the creature isn't constantly guarding?" I asked, pointing to marks on the map where there appeared to be windows or doors.

"I'm afraid Xudias cast a security spell on the house that's tied to some object in the house. Paranoid bastard was always taking extra precautions to prevent anyone from seeing what went on in there."

"So, the only way in is the front door? Where is the creature then?"

"…In the entrance hall," the captain admitted.

"By the front door? Are you kidding me? How are we supposed to get the surprise attack on this thing? I mean we need to surprise attack it, right? If we don't, we risk ending up like everyone else that just charged in there," I asked these questions mostly to myself as I tried to think of a plan. Then, an idea occurred to me.

"Look into the magic shops and enchanters in town and see if anyone has or can make an anti-magic sphere. I know they're super rare, but if anyone has one, that'll fix our problem of a good entrance," I suggested.

"We don't have the resources to pay for something like that, unfortunately, even if we do manage to find one," the captain scowled as he retorted.

"Can't you just ask them to borrow it?" I said, as my pitch raised higher.

The captain glared at me for a few moments, but eventually he sighed and straightened up. "Guards! Report for duty!" A stream of guards entered the tent, totaling about twenty of them. "Good! Now, you are going to go search for an item enchanted with an anti-magic field. If you manage to find one, ask the person who has it if you can borrow it. Beg if you must, but bring it back here," the captain ordered, then he dismissed all of them with a wave of a hand.

The guards ran back out of the tent and took off into the city to hopefully find what we needed. In the meantime, Melinai and I were instructed by the captain to relax until the item was found or word was given that one didn't exist in the city. It took all day, playing cards with Melinai and surprisingly Nomad as he propped up his cards on the ledge of the war table so he could read them, but we couldn't. Several of the games were very close, mostly between Nomad and Melinai, but in the end Nomad won every single one. Melinai and I collapsed after the last game, infuriated to lose to a dog, a magic dog, but still a dog. Just as Melinai and I were

116

licking our metaphorical wounds, a guard came rushing into the tent, clearly out of breath. He collapsed down onto one knee and held out a black and gold stone toward the captain as he panted. The captain who had been simply pacing behind the war table this entire time, finally walked around the table and approached the guard. He took the stone that the guard held out to him, and patted him on the shoulder.

"Good work. Now, go get some rest at the barracks," the captain said warmly. The guard nodded and slowly, painfully stood up and limped out of the tent. The captain waited for the guard to go, then he walked over to me and handed me the stone. "You know how to use that thing, right?"

I nodded, "Of course, I found one once on a quest. The thing paid for my house once I sold it!"

The captain nodded, satisfied, and returned to his place at the table. I began to work with the stone, putting my mana into it and detailing exactly the type of magic the field the stone created would cancel. These items had to have limiters put in when they were created, otherwise they would cancel all magic, even the mana in people's bodies. They were designed to get rid of only one type of magic at a time, and could never be used to take the mana from a living being. I assumed that it was a force field spell and made the stone ready to get rid of that type of magic once activated. Now all I could hope was that there weren't trap spells put on the windows as well. We then concocted a bit of a plan with the insight from the captain and set out to get the quest over with.

We snuck around the back to a first floor window that opened easily. I reached to try to find the forcefield and immediately jammed my hand against it as it was just inside the window frame. I then put some mana into the anti-magic stone and reached out once more. It worked like a charm, and the forcefield faded away temporarily. I used it to get Melinai and Nomad inside and then deactivated it by taking my mana back out of it. I looked at my two party members and nodded, it was go time. We snuck silently through the manor, down the two hallways and into the main hallway which I could tell led to the front door. We slipped past doorway after doorway until finally we made it to the entrance hall, a massive room with a very high ceiling and bodies that littered the floor. I looked around quickly, searching for a sign of the creature, but finding none, I motioned silently for Nomad and Melinai to begin to check the bodies for survivors. I stepped into the left side of the room where there sat a large dire bear rug that was in tatters, as it looked like something had cut it or stabbed it countless times.

I bent down to inspect the cuts more thoroughly when I heard what sounded like a wind chime coming from down the hall. I squinted into the darkness, trying to see where the sound was coming from when all of a sudden, a long, huge, and stringy blob of flesh carrying countless pieces of metal flew into the room, landing in the center, right in front of the door. We were separated now, with Nomad and Melinai on one side and me on the other. We had lost the element of surprise, so I unsheathed my sword and prepared for a harrowing battle. The creature in front of us began to take shape as more metal flew to its aide, forming its body until before us stood a giant metal owl. Seeing its true form, I quickly came to the conclusion that this thing was going to be doing physical attacks, not magical ones, so I put away my magic sword and took out two short swords which I spun in my hands for good measure before charging at the creature.

I flew up a good fifteen feet and allowed myself to drop out of the air down onto the owl with my swords pointed down. I felt my blades sink into the metal. I had succeeded in getting through the metal, but as I pulled my swords back out, I saw them to be badly damaged. "Shit," I cursed under my breath just as the owl reared back one of its legs and flapped its jagged metal wings, knocking me to the ground and nearly stepping on and crushing Melinai. I quickly flipped myself right-side up, and pulled out my handaxe. If I couldn't get through the metal without breaking my weapons, then I was just going to have to find some exposed flesh

118

on this thing. I flew up once more, this time flying all around it, searching for a weak spot as the owl continually tried to slice me out of the air with its wings.

Melinai began to play a song, and I felt my muscles fill with a kick of adrenaline. Nomad seemed to feel this effect as well, as he lunged for the bird's ankle, tearing into the metal. The owl tried to kick him off, but his bite was too strong and even as it lifted its leg up in the air, Nomad simply hung from it stubbornly. Seeing these two try their best, I knew I had to try my best as well. Not finding any weak points, I flew around to the front of this thing, right in its face, and let out a roar. The owl did just what I wanted, and took this as a challenge to which it replied with a terrible, ear-piercing screech. My head hurt and I felt blood trickle out of my ear holes, but I had gotten what I wanted, for when the owl screeched it revealed its weakness, a fleshy bundle at the very center of this thing's chest, slightly glowing with white light. If that wasn't a weak point, I didn't know what was, so I yelled at Melinai. "Mel! Can you paralyze this thing for a second? I only need a second. I'm going inside of it!"

"You're going to *what*?! And yes, I do, but are you sure now is the time to use it? I can only use it once!" Melinai shouted back as he dipped and dodged the claws and also tried to continue playing his lute.

"Do it!" I demanded, narrowly moving out of the way of a wing that was swung at me.

Melinai immediately obliged, and cast a powerful spell on his lute to freeze the owl in place. In the seconds after the owl froze, I dove forward, straight into its open mouth. The owl was so large I actually had room to fly around inside of it, but I didn't have long to gawk at this as it began to move once more. As if knowing that I was inside of it, every metal shard on the owl lifted up and pointed inwards, trying to pierce my flesh. I flew out of the way of one group of shards, only to accidentally slam into another. My armor protected me for the most part, but I was still wounded. I

119

gritted my teeth and pulled myself off of the spikes with great force before diving down to the creature's center. Once there, I lifted my hand axe, ready to destroy it when I noticed a fist-sized yellow egg under all of the flesh.

The kid's voice flashed in my mind, asking me if the creature was a monster because it was made. I shook my head at this, and went to strike it down anyway as more spikes pierced into me. But I couldn't get myself to do it. The more I thought about it, the more I believed that this thing may have just been a product of its master, and that it could still be saved, given a fresh start. I rolled my eyes at myself. "I'm too damn soft for this," I grumbled as I proceeded to carefully cut around the egg, getting rid of all the flesh attached to it. Once I did this, the owl began to fall to pieces. Metal rained down around and above me, and I got clipped by more than a few of them, though this time I didn't get any serious wounds. Back in the room, I took off my pack and wrapped the egg on some spare clothes I had brought, and tucked it away in my pack. I would figure out what to do with that later. For now, I needed some healing and some rest, so I went over and threw open the front door.

"The creature has been slain!" I lied triumphantly, not wanting them to take away the egg and destroy it.

The guards that were outside the manor cheered, and many began to rush into the building to look for survivors and reclaim the dead. As I stood outside, a healer ran over to me to treat my pierced flesh, and I sighed, relieved that no one had called me on my lie. That is until I felt someone push on my pack. I turned around and saw Nomad pointing his snout at my pack directly where I had put the egg. I began to panic and started to try to shoo him away, but nothing worked. Eventually, I resorted to bribery.

"What is it? Do you want a steak? Two massive steaks?" I offered in a hushed voice, but Nomad's eyes simply narrowed at me and he pushed on the pack again. "Ok? Well, what about

120

money? Do you even use money? Whatever, I'll give you two gold to drop this and walk away."

Nomad nodded and waited for me to give him his bribe. I pulled out the money and tossed it to him, expecting him to let them fall to the ground. Instead, however, he caught them in the air, and proceeded to *swallow* them. I cringed at the sight, but didn't say anything as he pranced off, wagging his tail. After the healer finished his work, I told Melinai that I'd meet him back at the tavern after I picked up the kid from the guildhall. He nodded and continued to play his lute while the healer tended to his wounds. I walked to the guildhall leisurely, thinking about how I would raise the creature in the egg, and how the kid would react to what I did. I hoped that she would be happy to know that I didn't blindly kill something that was similar to her. I arrived at the guildhall about twenty minutes later and as I walked in my heart froze as I saw Mika looking around in a panic.

I ran over to her and grabbed her hands in mine. "Mika! Mika, it's ok. When did you lose her?"

She whimpered and admitted quietly, "About forty minutes ago." Nomad was curling himself around her, whining worriedly as Mika shook and cried. "I'm so sorry, Luis! I tried, and I thought she'd be fine if I just took my eyes off her for just a second, but then she was gone."

I nodded and gave her hands a squeeze. "Nomad, can you help me track her down? And Mika, did she leave anything behind?"

Mika nodded and handed me the kid's veil, which she explained had fallen off of her when she ran away. Nomad on the other hand didn't seem to want to cooperate at first as he simply scoffed at me. But Mika turned to look at him, giving him what I assumed to be large begging eyes. Nomad furrowed his brow and sighed, but nodded nonetheless. I held out the veil for Nomad to get the scent off of, and he took off running. He was much faster than me, so I decided to fly over the streets, which was generally frowned upon since it could easily lead to in-air accidents. I didn't care about any trouble I would get into, all I cared about was making sure the kid was safe, so I flew, following Nomad as he bounded through the streets, not caring that he was knocking over people as he went. Eventually, he stopped in front of what appeared to be a temple, and I quickly landed next to him.

"This the place?" I asked, and he gave a short nod.

I didn't waste any time, as I sprinted into the building. Inside, there was a single priest, but no sign of the kid. I looked around and saw a slightly open door, I didn't pause and ran straight through, even as the priest tried to stop me. Once inside, I looked around wildly, but finally saw her standing next to another priest. I ran down the stairs, skipping every other step, and went right up to her; sweeping her up and into a hug.

"Kid, listen. I'm not mad, but why did you leave the guildhall? You know I told you that you'd be safe there with Mika."

The kid looked guilty and embarrassed, but spoke up after a moment. "I'm sorry, I got worried about you when you never came back...I thought maybe you needed my help."

If I was the least bit irritated by her running away before, that was all gone now. "That is very sweet of you, but I'm *your* guardian. Not the other way around. So, no more running off when I tell you to stay somewhere, ok?"

She nodded and smiled then sighed, "I'm glad you're safe, though."

I pinched her cheek and chuckled. "That's *my* line!"

She giggled and pinched my cheek right back, "Just because you have to worry about me doesn't mean I can't worry about you."

"Alright, alright. But I am glad you're safe. Did anything happen, or have you just been relaxing here the whole time?" I joked, expecting the answer to be the latter. The kid looked off to the side, and then proceeded to tell me about the men who assaulted her. My blood felt like it was boiling in my veins I was so angry. "Kid, I'm going to need exact descriptions of what they looked like," I said in a low growl.

She stayed silent for a moment, but then spoke up in a quiet voice, "But they didn't know."

"Kid! No! Even if you were a golem, that would be unacceptable. Those assholes need to be taught a lesson." I cracked my knuckles and stood up. "Now, what did they look like?"

She gave me as detailed of descriptions as she could remember, and honestly I was impressed she was able to take such note of their appearances while being so scared. I took mental notes on everything she said, and planned on talking to the guards about them later. Afterwards, she gestured to the priest next to her.

"Oh by the way, this is Margub. He helped me when I had no place to go," she explained with a smile that betrayed some embarrassment.

I looked to him with slight surprise, as I was so focused on her that I forgot he existed. "Oh, well I can't thank you enough for giving the kid a safe place to stay." I held out my hand to shake his.

Margub grabbed the inside of my forearm, a greeting most commonly seen in Fae cultures, but a little strange to see in Aethos. "No need, my child. I'm just happy I could help." He then leaned down a bit to get eye level with the kid. "And please do know that you are welcome here in any times of need that you may encounter."

She nodded and smiled, and then looked back to me. "Ready? We need to go back to the guildhall before Mika has a heart attack over you," I chuckled and reached out a hand to her, which she promptly took.

From there, we walked out of the library and then out of the temple altogether. On the outside, Nomad sat on the front steps of the temple, spraying water at random passerby and snickering to himself. We walked down the steps around him, and as we did so, I sighed as I saw him stare at me expectantly. I reached into my coin pouch and handed him one more gold coin which he promptly swallowed. The kid stared at this display in shock, but quickly recovered, giggling as Nomad sprayed her lightly in the face with some water.

Chapter 14:

What a Wonderful Life It Is

Luis, Nomad, and I walked back to the guild in the soft light of the street lamps, passing by few people until we got back on the main road where there still were large crowds. Many weren't going into stores or buying at the market, but rather enjoying the night life of food and performers that dotted the streets with music and dance. The tavern was the busiest of anything though, with over a hundred people lined up outside of it, waiting for their turn to get in and drink. We were going to the guildhall for now though, and headed inside. The hall was much more lively than it was before, with many people drinking and eating at the many tables and the bar. As soon as we walked in, Mika dashed towards us and pulled me into a hug.

"Are you ok? You're not hurt? I'm so sorry I made you want to leave! I should've paid you more attention or given you something to do. Oh this is all my fault!" she rambled as she held me tightly.

"It's ok! It's not your fault! I just got worried about Luis. I thought I needed to go help him," I admitted quietly, my face burning as I pulled away from her hug.

Mika stood up straight and put her hands on her hips as she glared at Luis. "How could you give her the delusion that she could possibly help you in a battle with a deadly monster?!" she scolded him harshly. "You know what this means right? You're going to have to train her, so that if she gets that feeling again, she can actually protect herself. She'll start her training first thing tomorrow morning, and you'll be helping me train her, so don't think you can just drop her off!"

125

I looked up to Luis helplessly, not knowing how to feel about being signed up for training all of a sudden without my consent. Luis stared down at me just as helplessly and shrugged.

"Good! Oh, and Luis, your reward for the quest will be ready tomorrow, I imagine the city is going to pay you pretty well. Now go get some rest, you're going to need it!" Mika ushered Luis and me out the door and promptly closed it behind us.

"Welp, looks like you're going to start training! Yay!" he said weakly. "I'm sorry she dragged you into this, she's a little overzealous sometimes."

I smiled and shook my head "It's ok. Besides, I *would* like to be able to help you on quests, so I don't mind!"

Luis put his arm around my shoulders and pulled me into a half hug as we walked, letting go as we entered the tavern. Inside, everyone ate, drank, laughed, and even danced to the band. Melinai was among the patrons, drinking and singing along with the crowd. He almost didn't notice us, even from his unsteady perch standing on a chair, but eventually he saw us as Luis waved largely to him. Having just had a bad experience with drunk men specifically, I flinched slightly as he approached us. Thankfully, Melinai was too drunk to notice, and began talking to Luis about their grand quest. He prattled on, recounting every detail and explaining how each one would show up as lyrics in the "amazing" song he was writing. Luis managed to get Melinai to go back to his drinks and singing, and then we headed up to the room at Luis's request.

Luis sat down on his bed and gestured for me to sit across from him on mine before reaching into his pack and pulling out a book. It was the same one he had started reading to me before we left for Cadmar, and he smiled as he suggested that we finish it. I nodded, and got comfortable on the bed, sitting cross-legged and pulling the blanket around me. As Luis started to read aloud, I suddenly realized that he was not only skipping dinner but skipping being around his friends in order to do this. I was about to speak up when another realization dawned on me, Luis was likely doing this because he noticed me flinch at being around Melinai and all the other drunkards in the tavern. I pulled the edges of the blanket tightly around me as my head filled with butterflies.

The story of the Hegal boy in the Angel city continued with the boy meeting his first friend, an Angel that he saved from some boys that were bullying her. The boy ended up getting pretty badly beaten because of it, but the girl was unscathed. The boy expected the girl to run off or treat him horribly like everyone else did, but instead she helped him tend to his wounds, using a little bit of healing magic to ease the pain of the worst ones. From there, the two grew up together, both of them facing opposition to their friendship along the way, but both of them spiting in the face of that opposition. Eventually, the girl and boy fell in love, but knew that the girl's family would forbid them to ever be together. So, the two packed up their things and ran away together.

Everything was perfect at first, they had made their home out in the wilderness, away from everyone, and they were happy. But then, the girl's family found the two and their little house, and caught it ablaze in the middle of the night while the two were sleeping. The boy was unaffected by the flames because of his Demon ancestry, but the girl was mortally wounded by the flames. When the boy eventually woke up and saw his love wounded so, he screamed that he would kill every last person responsible for this. But before he could leave, the girl called out to him. "Do not become the monster they believe you to be," were her last words, and though he desperately wanted revenge, he listened to the words of his lost love and simply tried to move on with his life.

I cried as the last scene played out, and even Luis had to swipe away some tears from his eyes as he read it. It was very late by the time we finished reading, so late in fact that Melinai came stumbling into the room and collapsed onto his cot. Luis and I laughed at the sudden entrance, but then decided that it'd be best to get some rest and talk about our feelings about the book later the next day. We both curled up in our respective beds and immediately fell to sleep.

127

The next morning was hectic, as Luis woke me up an hour before sunrise to get ready to go train. Thankfully, my body couldn't feel unrested since sleep was optional, but I still felt uncomfortable mentally for getting so little sleep. The two of us bid Melinai goodbye, and went downstairs where Luis inhaled a quick breakfast. From there, we went straight to the guildhall, which as we entered Mika stood from her chair and marched over to us.

"Only twenty minutes early? I expect at least thirty from you both in the future," Mika demanded as she closed a small metal disk with a lid that was attached to a chain at her hip. I pointed to it curiously, and she smiled and held it out so I could see. "It's called a clock. Brand new and very expensive, but also very handy for telling time! You like it? I got mine in silver," she boasted and opened and closed it several times to show it off.

I was fascinated by it. A metal disk that tells time? Even my old memories seemed to have no idea what it was. But I couldn't admire it for long, as Mika put it back in her pocket and clapped her hands.

"Now, first things first. You can't train in a dress, so I had someone find some leather armor and regular clothes in your size. So, take these and go get dressed in the bathrooms." She handed me the clothes and armor and I headed over to where she instructed me to go to find the bathrooms and change there.

I had never worn armor before, so putting it on was a bit challenging, but I eventually somewhat figured it out. I walked back over to Mika and Luis, dressed in the new clothes and armor, and smiled awkwardly as moving in leather armor was certainly an experience I wasn't used to. Mika looked me up and down and nodded before guiding me through the back hall to the back door which exited onto the training ground. Luis followed close behind and gave me a gentle shove as I hesitated to go through the door. Once outside, Mika and Luis began to discuss amongst themselves what type of adventurer I should be. Luis was dead set on me being a fighter like him, but Mika was more of the mindset of training me

128

in several disciplines to better prepare me for any situation. They bickered for a few moments until Mika turned to look at me.

"Kid, do you know any magic?" Mika asked.

"No, she-" Luis began, but Mika held a finger up to his lips.

"I want to hear it from her," Mika said in a stern tone as though scolding him.

The first thing that came to mind was my experience with the drunken men and how I had saved myself, so I quietly explained the situation that had occurred to Mika. Luis looked shocked, as I had never told him how I got away. Mika smiled triumphantly at first, but then saw how I acted about recounting the tale, and immediately apologized that I had had to go through it.

"But regardless, that means you have an innate individual magic of fire. So, your training will be in two parts, exercising and training with a weapon, and then learning and practicing fire magic. Sound good?" Mika asked, though she did so in a way that implied it was rhetorical.

After Luis and Mika bickered a bit more, Luis relented, and agreed to Mika's training regimen for me. He insisted on being the one to teach me weapon fighting, while Mika would handle the magic training. We started with weapons training, and Luis took me over to a shed that was full to the brim with weapons of every kind. He instructed me to pick one, and that that would be the weapon I trained with from then on. I tested the weight and feeling of several weapons, but none of them piqued my interest until I saw one at the back of the shed. I scooted in sideways past many of the weapons, and snatched up the one that had caught my eye. I came back out of the shed, displaying it proudly. It was a spear with a curved tip, and it was just my size, not too big and not too small.

After picking the spear as my chosen weapon, Luis started off my training by having me practice carrying it around on my back and in my hands through obstacles and exercises. This was what we did for several hours until lunch time. Luis and Mika took the chance to eat, and then Mika began her training of me in magic. Her training consisted of memorizing all of the runes and their uses. This too lasted several hours, until sunset. My brain felt fried, but I was enjoying the training as I felt like I was making something of myself and starting a new journey.

A month of training passed by in the blink of an eye, and I spent much of the last few days before that month ended sparring with Luis, Mika, and several others from the guild that volunteered to help out. I wasn't brilliant, but with my magic and my spear and shield, I was able to actually stand a chance against my sparring partners. I even won a match against a newcomer to the guild that had been in training about a month longer than me. After winning said match, Mika decided it was time to send me on my first quest. It would be pretty simple, not very dangerous, and Luis would be following me just in case, but I was excited nonetheless.

I was sent on my first quest to clear out some magically mutated rats from the sewer system below the city on an early August morning. It was raining that morning, but that didn't bother Luis or me since we'd soon be underground anyway. We made our way to a large grate in the ground, and we had a guard meet us there in order to unlock the lock that kept the grate in place. As soon as it was unlocked, Luis lifted up the grate and we climbed down into the muck of the sewers. I jumped off of the ladder over to the walkway next to the sewage, and Luis followed right after me after I moved out of the way. We patrolled the sewers in search of the rats for a good hour, only ever finding normal rats that we let skitter away from our lantern light. We were about to give up when something occurred to me, and I quickly began to draw out the runes in the air.

I forgot that I had learned how to scry with fire, so I quickly scried for the mutated rats in the flame of the lantern. It took a few moments of searching, but eventually I saw a path from where we were to the rats. I took off down the tunnel, with Luis jogging after me, ready for my first real quest to reach its climax. I ran through the tunnel until finally I came face to face with three rats, each one about three feet tall and all of them bearing some sort of markings, someone had forcefully mutated them. But that wasn't what stopped me dead in my tracks, for when the rats reared back at the sight of the lantern light, they revealed what they had been eating, a Human body. I couldn't move and my mind was frozen, I could see the face, a young girl; no one I knew and yet I could only see Her face, the face of who I was before.

One of the rats began to lunge at me, and Luis called out to me to get me to snap out of it. I quickly blocked the rat's attack with my shield and set down the lantern before unsheathing my dagger. Unfortunately, I couldn't bring my spear with me since the ceilings of the tunnels were too low, but I had trained with a dagger enough to at least know how to attack with it. So as the rat reared up on its hind legs, ready to lunge again, I struck forth, sinking the dagger into its flesh, and then dragging it quickly downwards and jerking to the left. The rat fell dead. The other two rats both reared up, one looking like it was going to lunge at me while the other began to cast a spell in my direction. I blocked the lunge attack again with my shield, and hastily drew out the runes in the air for a counterspell with my other hand. The magic the rat had been casting fizzled away as my counterspell worked perfectly. Nodding in a silent victory, I pushed back on the rat with my shield, sending it stumbling back a few steps. Before it could recover, I slashed my dagger at its throat, and it too fell dead. The last rat shrieked and began to run off, but it didn't get far before I cast a ball of fire at it that charred it to a crisp.

The fight now over, Luis picked up the lantern and patted me on the shoulder. "Good work. I'll get some guards down here to collect the body of whoever these things ate, but for now, your quest is done! Go ahead and head back to the guildhall, I'll meet you there."

I nodded and went to turn away to move down the tunnel, but my eyes caught on the face of the body once more. *It's not the same, I don't know that person* I scolded myself, and turned away fully this time as I went to head back to the grate and out of the sewers. As I walked back to the guildhall, I silently cursed myself that I had gotten hung up on those memories. I had an amazing life now, I shouldn't have been held back like that. The past was gone and couldn't get me anymore. That's what I told myself.

Back at the guildhall, Mika and several other guild members greeted me warmly, insisting to hear every detail of how my first quest went. I was still caught up on the image of that body, so I kept my description fairly vague, only really focusing on the part where I killed the rats. Mika and the others cheered and patted me on the back, and then Mika rewarded me with my payment for the quest: five silver coins. I treasured these, and put them into the coin pouch Luis had gotten me earlier that month. This little bit of excitement and happiness made it easier to not think about the sewers, but my mind still lingered there on occasion. After Luis and I met up, we headed back to the tavern where Luis spent some time drinking and talking with Melinai and other patrons of the bar, and I spent time taking a nap in the room.

In my dreams, I lay on the cold stone floors of the sewers, Richard's sobs echoing through the tunnels, but I couldn't tell from where. All I could see, or feel were the rats tearing at my flesh, sending me off to the underworld with a gruesome display of carnage. I woke up with a slight scream several hours later just as Richard's sobs grew closer and closer. Thankfully, Luis and Melinai were still at the bar, and I didn't have to worry about explaining the horrid nightmare I had just had. I didn't want to go back to sleep, but I couldn't bring myself to go be around people at that moment, so I simply curled up in the fetal position on my cot and began to hum to myself the song Luis had taught me.

The door opened about an hour later, and I sat up to see Luis, who went over to his pack and peered inside to check on his gear like he did several times a day. This time though he gasped excitedly, and reached inside before carefully pulling out a large, yellow egg. It dawned on me in that moment that the entirety of the month, every time he told me he was checking on his gear, he

132

had actually been checking on this egg. I stood from the cot and went over to look at the egg, which was beginning to slowly pip open. As it struggled to open, Luis explained to me that he had gotten it from the metal creature he had defeated. I smiled with a warm feeling in my chest, he had listened to me all that time ago when I had asked if it was a monster or not simply because it was made.

We watched the egg in anticipation for several minutes, until finally, a small circle had been broken open and the creature inside pushed it up and off of the egg entirely. Inside, there was an amorphous blob of flesh that reached up and out. Luis told me to hold out my hands, and then proceeded to gently tip the creature out of the egg and into my hands. It jiggled there in my hands for a moment before a small eye blinked open and raised up from the rest of the blob on a small, fleshy stalk. It blinked at me slowly and made a series of chirping sounds, and I giggled as I watched it wiggle around. But then I looked at the creature closely, and it occurred to me that it may have been wiggling because it wanted something. Knowing that this creature was usually surrounded by metal, I carefully moved the creature into one of my hands and then went over to Luis's pack. Just as I suspected, he had a damaged short sword still tucked away in his pack. I reached in and pulled it out as Luis watched me, confused. Sword now in hand, I gently touched the middle of the sword to the blob of flesh. My guess was correct as the sword split into a million tiny shards of metal that wrapped around the blob, forming it a body. The body was that of a small baby owl, and I smiled happily that I had guessed correctly.

"Welp, I'm never getting that sword back, am I?" Luis chuckled and patted the metal owl gently on its head with one finger.

Chapter 15:

Heading Home

During the month that the kid was training, I took some quests within Cadmar, and Mika paid me a little for my help with training. With both of those incomes, I was able to take care of me and the kid, while Melinai took care of himself by playing nightly shows at the tavern. I would've been content to stay in Cadmar for as long as training the kid took, but when the egg hatched, it changed everything. The kid didn't want to leave the creature in the room, and insisted on it being by her side at all times. This was difficult given that any guard or Mika that saw it would know what I had done. So, we decided to pack up and head back home to Tithridge.

But not before we spent a little time in the city, seeing the sights. The kid had spent the entire month training and studying at every waking moment that she hadn't really had the chance to see any of the things that made Cadmar amazing. So, I decided to splurge a little bit, and bought me and the kid tickets to see the current running play at the theater. Melinai agreed to watch the creature for the kid while we were gone, but he did give me a disapproving glare when I first showed it to him. Over at the theatre, we saw a morning showing of the play, *A Lily in the Valley*. It was an older play about two star-crossed lovers who went through many challenges together, but ended up breaking up after their families forbade their union. The final scene was of the lovers enchanting a white lily at the place they always used to meet to remind them and others of their love.

The play was amazing, from the costumes to the acting, it was perfect. I found myself fondly admiring the art the performers had created and took the chance to throw a rose I bought to them at curtain call. After the play, it was still before noon, and we didn't plan on leaving until closer to three o'clock. To pass the time, we enjoyed the performers of Cadmar, watching minstrels play songs, acrobats do tricks, and artists paint their masterpieces. Eventually, we made our way over to a large area of the street where many people were drawing on the stones with chalk. This immediately piqued the kid's interest, and she insisted on buying a piece of chalk so that she could try her hand at drawing. I paid the salesman there a copper and got a large piece of chalk that I handed off to the kid.

"Let's see what you've got!" I encouraged her, and she nodded, determined.

She started small with a singular flower that she put great detail into, but then it blossomed into a spiral design of dancing blooms. When she was done about an hour later, she stood up and looked over her work with satisfaction. It certainly wasn't the best piece there, but it was far from the worst, and I patted her on the back in celebration of her hard work. She smiled up at me brightly, and I could swear I saw the kid's eyes sparkle. After that, it was finally time to head out, so we went and picked up our things and the creature at the tavern. We parted ways with Melinai after he performed his song about our quest for us one last time.

We left Cadmar that day with little notice to Mika, simply leaving a letter. We snuck the creature out of the city in my pack, and once we were out of the piercing gaze of the guards, we let it out. It screeched a complaint as it landed on the kid's shoulder. As we traveled, the kid tried several times to feed it food from my rations, but it refused to take it. It didn't seem to complain of hunger either, though, so we assumed that it merely fed off of mana. The kid and I were talking about the play as we traveled, and we both nearly had heart attacks as the creature blurted out the word "Lily" after the kid had said it.

"It can talk?!" I said in horror.

"It can talk!" the kid said with glee.

The creature seemed to pick up on the kid's excitement and jumped up and down on her shoulder several times as it said "Lily" over and over again.

"Well, that settles it. I think it just chose its name for us," I said as I chuckled.

The kid nodded in agreement and proceeded to spend the rest of the hour before sunset trying to teach Lily new words. Lily caught on pretty quickly, and it made me wonder why the monster version of this thing hadn't tried to talk to us. I shrugged this off, though, and focused on the road ahead until sunset fell over the land. Once the light had gone from around us, we set up camp for the night and got settled in our respective bedrolls. Lily curled up inside the kid's of course, and we all slept soundly through the night. The next few days until getting to Swindon were spent with me and the kid slowly teaching Lily more and more words. At one point, I even managed to teach it how to whistle a tune.

Something occurred to me as we reached the border of Swindon, though, and I brought it up with the kid. "You really like Lily, right?"

The kid nodded, a bit confused as to why I was asking, though.

"Then why don't we get her soul-bound to you?" I suggested.

The kid seemed to know what that was as she immediately looked excited and hurriedly asked Lily if that's what she wanted as well. There were several minutes of the kid explaining what being soul bound means, but eventually Lily agreed whole-heartedly.

"Great, then it's a good thing we're in Swindon since here is the only place I know someone who has experience with soul-binding," I explained as I guided her to the tavern.

Once inside, everyone greeted us cheerily, and Vel in particular waved one of her four arms to get my attention.

"Welcome back, Luis! Though if I'm honest I didn't expect you back so soon. You usually take at least a couple of months every time you go to Cadmar," Vel filled up a beer mug with one set of her arms and set it in front of me heavily.

"Yeah, well there was no real need for me to stick around this time. Anyway, Vel do you happen to know where old man Poe is?"

Vel clicked her tongue. "Where else?" She then gestured to a table in the back left of the tavern next to the small stage.

I grabbed the beer and tapped on the bar with my other hand twice in thanks as I smiled and winked at her. I headed straight up to the old man who was slumped in his chair, clearly drunk out of his mind. He was a Water Elemental whose creator had died many years ago. With no one to serve, and a vast supply of gold left to him by his creator, he had always said he had no reason to not drink his days away. I set the mug in front of Poe on the table heavy enough to get his attention, but not enough to spill its contents. Poe looked up at the mug slowly, his eyes dark and lacking life, and darted forward, reaching for the handle. I let go of the mug just in time as Poe proceeded to down the beer in a few quick gulps before sighing and looking up at me.

"What can I- *hic* do you for, Luis?" Poe slurred through the sentence.

"Well Poe, I need your help. We-" I started, but instantly got interrupted by Poe.

"The mighty Luis Rockwell needs *my* help? I never thought I'd see the day," Poe teased, reaching up to playfully punch my arm.

I cleared my throat awkwardly. "Yes, well, you're the only person I know in Swindon or Tithridge that knows how to do a soul-binding. Would-"

He cut me off again, this time with a dark expression. "Nope, absolutely not! I'm a free man, you hear me? Free to drink till the end of days or the end of gold, whichever comes first!"

I narrowed my eyes and raised my eyebrows. "Really, Poe?" I sighed heavily and rubbed my forehead. "I'm not here to soul-bind *you*! I want you to soul bind the kid and her bird."

Poe looked surprised at the kid and Lily. "Weird bird…Why's it got only one eye? Wait, is that kid a candle? What's going on here?! Did I finally drink so much I ascended from the normal plane of reality?" Poe blabbered.

"Never mind any of that, can you do the soul-binding for them? Please?" I asked sternly as I grabbed him by the shoulders.

"Oh, yeah I can do that. Follow me!" Poe said boisterously as he teetered his way out of the tavern.

Once outside, we followed Poe to the west side of the village where there sat a largely abandoned manor. The manor was a strange sight in this small farming village, but it had been there for many generations, and I fondly remembered playing in the overgrown gardens there when I was a kid. We walked up to the door with Poe as he unlocked the heavy oaken doors and swung them open haphazardly, gesturing for us to go in. We walked into the entrance hall, a large area with a huge chandelier that was covered in cobwebs and dust. In fact, as we walked through the

138

hall, it became apparent that *everything* was covered in cobwebs and dust. Poe jogged over to get in front of us, and bowed sloppily as he gestured for us to head off to the left into a lounge room. This room was still pretty disheveled like the rest of the house, but unlike the other rooms, this one looked lived in to a degree, with used pillows and blankets crumpled on one of the couches.

"Wait here, I've got to go get the book," Poe mumbled as he left us in the room.

The kid and I got settled onto the couch that didn't look like it was used as Poe's bed and waited patiently in silence. I listened to the gentle creaking of the house while the kid spoke quietly to Lily, still insisting on teaching her some more new words. A few minutes passed, when Poe came stumbling back into the room, a large book in his hands. He set it down heavily on the coffee table in front of us, causing dust to go flying everywhere. I waved my hands in the air to disperse the dust, but I still ended up sneezing a few times.

"Page two-hundred and three. Just draw the runes and read through that spell out loud while you hold the bird in your hand," Poe instructed as he collapsed onto the opposite couch where he promptly fell to sleep.

I shook my head in disappointment, but the kid got right to work, and opened the book up to the correct page. She held Lily carefully in one hand and traced the spell's runes in the air with the other as she began to recite the spell. It only took her a few moments, and when the spell was finished, both the kid and Lily glowed a bright white for a split second. I flinched and snapped my eyes shut at the flash, but when the kid touched my shoulder, I opened my eyes slowly. Lily had perched back on the kid's shoulder and the kid looked up at me worriedly. I waved my hand dismissively and told her I was fine as I stood and offered her my other hand. She smiled and took my hand, standing carefully and then dusting off her dress. Lily seemed to share a look with the kid, but I didn't think much of it, and we headed out of the manor after I set two silver coins on the table for Poe. That would buy him a few drinks at least, and hopefully he would see it as a fair trade for helping us out. If not, then I would repay him next time I was in Swindon.

We went back to the tavern for the night since there was only an hour left before sunset. I had a nice meal of some mutton and rice, while the kid munched on one of her candles. In the morning, we set out just before sunrise, and I ate breakfast on the road. The kid continued teaching Lily how to speak, and seemed to never get tired of it, even as Lily would mess up or need a word to be repeated at least a dozen times. While we were walking that day, we walked over a hill and were greeted by the sight of a giant snail pulling a small house on wheels. The snail was taller than me by about three feet and moved surprisingly fast. Well, as fast as a walking horse, but still faster than I had assumed giant snails to move. Lily immediately flew over to it to check it out, and we walked over to catch up with her. Lily had apparently found the rider of this wagon house, as she sat on his arm and repeated the word 'friend' over and over. The rider was a Gnome man, his giant mouse ears hanging out rather than being tucked up inside a hat like most Gnomes had them.

"Hello there! Is this little fellow yours?" the man asked and gestured with the arm that Lily was perched on as we approached him.

The kid nodded, and whistled for Lily to come back to her, which she did immediately.

"Heading to Cadmar?" I asked the man.

"That's right! And then on to Albern for the magic festival!" the man threw his hands into the air causing a shower of sparks to spring forth from his fingertips.

"Oh, is it that time of year again? Shame I can't make it this year. I always love to see the shows people put on," I said as I reminisced on the two years I had been to the festival.

"Ah, a shame indeed! Where are you heading to then? On to Alya or perhaps over to Shelland?" The man leaned in to look at us closer.

"Nope, to Tithridge, actually. We live there," I explained.

The man raised his eyebrows. "I see many people that pass through Tithridge to get to the cities it is between, but it is not often I meet someone from there. Other than the store owners, I mean."

I shrugged and changed the subject, "Well, we better get going, we've got a long few more days of travel ahead of us."

"Righty o' then! Good luck and safe travels!" The man bowed his head slightly and then his snail began to move once more.

We waved as he left, and then continued down the road. The next few days were wholly uneventful, until the last day, that is. On the last day before we arrived back in Tithridge, we were passing by the same grove of trees I had gotten my honey from before. I considered going to get some again, but the kid gave me a disapproving look, so I decided against it. I was content to keep going right past it, but Lily suddenly flew off of the kid's shoulder and into the trees. I was pondering why, considering the possibility that maybe she too liked honey for some reason, when she promptly returned carrying a flower in her beak. She dropped the flower into the kid's hands and then landed back on her shoulder. The kid examined the flower, an iris, carefully, trying to figure out why Lily had brought it to her.

I was wondering this too, when a thought occurred to me, "You know, your eyes are the exact same color as an iris."

"Are they?" she asked, looking at the flower more closely now.

"Hey there's an idea! Why not make your name something like that. You could go direct, and do just Iris, or you could go slightly off from that and do like Idris or Ipris or something," I suggested casually, not really thinking she'd agree.

"Which one do you like best?" she asked after a long pause.

I thought for a moment and then nodded to myself. "Yep, I like Ipris much better than the other options." I looked over to the kid who was deep in thought. "But you don't have to choose it! It's just a suggestion, something to get your brain working in the direction of actually picking a name," I blabbered nervously, thinking she might be offended that I had tried to pick her name for her.

"I like it," she whispered at first. She then looked up to me and said with confidence, "My name is Ipris!"

Chapter 16:

A Battle of Feelings

When we arrived back in Tithridge, it was nearly sunset and Luis was exhausted, so we decided to spend a night at the tavern and head home the next day. Entering the tavern, Luis immediately spotted Juli sitting at the bar, enjoying a drink by herself as she talked with the bartender. The skin under his scales turned beet red, and he looked at her like she was a goddess. My heart sank with the realization that the reason he was always so nervous around her was because he liked her. I felt like my stomach was dissolving my heart when I remembered what Margub had said to me, and I bolstered my courage that I could still have a chance. For now, though, Juli was still my friend and I had missed her, so I headed over with Luis to the bar where Juli greeted us both with hugs.

"Did you get any knitting done while you were gone?" Juli asked like she already knew the answer was no.

I shook my head. "I did learn how to fight and use magic though! I even went on a quest!" I said proudly.

Juli looked disapprovingly to Luis. "You know you shouldn't be making her take on *your* lifestyle and hobbies. She should be free to choose whatever hobbies she wants!"

Luis flinched at her cold stare and I giggled as I explained, "No, no. It's so I can protect myself! I had a run-in with some drunkards, and the guild leader and Luis thought it would be good to make it so that I can protect myself." I lied by leaving out the fact that it was so Luis could take me on quests and so that I could help him in battle.

Juli gave me the side eye as she was skeptical, but nodded after a moment when I smiled at her. "Well, what element of magic did you learn?"

"Fire!" I demonstrated by tracing a quick rune in the air and conjuring a flame above the tip of my pointer finger.

Juli clapped at first, but then looked at me confused. "Would that not melt you?" She leaned in to look at the tip of my finger to see if it was melting or not.

I shook my head. "When it's my fire, it doesn't do anything to me!" I demonstrated by shoving my other hand directly in the flame.

Juli was about to say something, but the bartender, a Zahhak, humanoid with reptilian characteristics, called over to us. "Hey! No fire magic in the bar! Don't want this place going up in flames!"

Juli snickered quietly as I hurried to snuff the flame. "Old Ugnro uses fire magic himself, but always insists that everyone else not use it in the bar. There's a lot of alcohol in here, so fair, but also hypocritical," she whispered as she leaned in close to my ear. Juli then leaned back smiling wide, and turned to Luis. "So, are you guys going to join me for a drink or are you heading home?"

Luis smiled bashfully. "W-We'll join you."

Juli chugged the rest of her drink, and then called out to the bartender. "Ugnro, two spiced meads over to that table!" She pointed to an empty table on the left side of the bar, which she then got up and headed over to, Luis and I following close behind. "So, what's that little bird thing on your shoulder, kid?"

144

"This is Lily, she's soul-bound to me," I explained as I held up a finger to Lily who rubbed up against it lovingly. "Oh! And she can speak!" I looked to Lily and gestured to Juli. "Lily, this is Juli. She's a friend."

Lily tilted her head and repeated back the word "friend" questioningly. I nodded, and Lily flew over to Juli's shoulder squawking "friend" over and over again. Juli giggled and pet Lily with one finger to which Lily closed her eyes happily letting Juli pet her. I called Lily back over to me after a few moments, to which she quickly obeyed, landing on my shoulder. Juli looked at me and Lily fondly, and I smiled back at her until something popped into my mind.

"Oh, by the way, I have a name now! It's Ipris! Luis and Lily helped me pick it," I said looking at Lily and then Luis with a smile.

Something crossed over Juli's face before she smiled at me, but I couldn't tell what it was. "That's a lovely name! It is nice to meet you again, Ipris." She took my hand in hers as she said this and gave it a gentle squeeze before letting go and beginning to talk with Luis about the details of his quest.

Luis and Juli talked for about an hour, catching up on everything each had missed while they were separated, after which Luis and I went up to our room in the tavern while Juli went home. In the morning, Luis and I awoke in our cots to the sound of a knock on our door. Luis got up and groggily answered the door, leaning up against the door frame and squinting into the light as he did so. On the other side, I heard Juli's voice.

"Now that you're back in town, why don't we take Ipris to the river? We can fish and swim! It'll be great!" Juli more insisted than suggested as she was already pushing her way into the room. Luis gave a quiet groan and Juli shot a glare at him. She walked into the room carrying a myriad of fishing supplies and made her way over to where I still lay in bed.

"Wakey, wakey, sunshine. We're going to the river!" Juli whispered excitedly.

I giggled and got out of bed, putting on my boots. Juli gave me a thumbs up and then hurried Luis and me out the door. From there, we walked west out of the village for a good hour until we finally arrived at the river. It was a fairly large river, spanning about one hundred feet wide, and there was a sturdy wooden bridge built across it. Juli led us over to a tree that sat next to the river and set everything down beneath the shade of it. She then began to set up the fishing rods, putting the line, hook, and bait on each one. Once they were all ready, she handed one to each of us, and led us back over to the bridge which she walked to the middle of and cast her line. Luis and I followed her example, though not getting too close to each other so our lines didn't cross. We fished like this for about three hours, and in that time, Luis caught two fish, I caught five, and Juli caught ten. Each time one of us caught something, Juli would have us put it in the basket she had brought so we could carry them home. After we had caught all of those fish, Juli decided it was time for swimming. I couldn't go too deep in the water since I didn't want my veil getting washed away, but I enjoyed the cool water on my feet as I sat on the river's edge.

Juli, on the other hand, was frolicking in the water, even in the deepest parts of the river. Luis watched her in awe for a little while until Juli ran up to him and dragged him in as well. The two played and joked in the water while I watched on, mostly paying attention to Lily who I had instructed to try to catch some fish of her own, even though she couldn't actually eat them. Lily returned a few times with mostly tiny fish which I had her return to the river, but eventually she managed to catch one that was about seven inches long. I applauded her and as I pet her I gave her some of my mana to which she squawked happily. I looked back out at Luis and

146

Juli and saw they were laying down a few feet apart from one another in a shallow part of the water, talking amongst themselves. I couldn't hear anything over the sounds of the river's current, but I assumed them to be talking about Luis's time in Cadmar again.

I shrugged and lay back on the grass, with Lily curling up in the crook of my arm, and took a nap. I awoke at sunset several hours later by Juli gently shaking me awake.

"Time to go!" She smiled wide and helped me to my feet.

Lily, still half asleep, flew lazily up to my shoulder, though she got tangled in my veil for a moment. I helped her get untangled as we walked back towards the village. Once we returned to Tithridge, I expected that Luis and I would finally head home, but Juli suddenly invited us over to her house. Luis of course agreed. We walked behind the market and shop section of the village and into the scattered residential area. We then went past this where there was a large plot of land brimming with flowers and a small house in the center. The entire plot was surrounded with a waist-high fence and a slightly taller gate at the front. When we walked up to the gate, Juli drew some runes on the wood of the gate with her finger and muttered an incantation. We watched as an invisible force field became visible for a split second and then dissolved into the air. Juli opened the gate and motioned for us to enter. After we walked through the gate, she quickly put the forcefield back up.

"Sorry about that. Gotta protect my stock, ya know?" She chuckled awkwardly and then went to open the front door for us.

Inside, the house was slightly smaller than Luis's, though unlike Luis's, it appeared to have a dining room instead of a lounge. She motioned to the table and began to light the lanterns in the room, insisting that we sit while she cooked. We did so, with Luis resting his head on the table for that little while as he seemed to be exhausted after fishing and swimming all day. I watched him rest peacefully, and as I did, I felt the urge to pat his head. My hand was halfway across the table as I realized that that would be too affectionate for our current relationship, and I snatched my hand back. Lily hopped from my shoulder down to the table and stared up at me curiously. I shook my head to dismiss her questioning, but this only served to make her more insistent as she looked back and forth between Luis and me. I blushed and shook my head again. This time I swear I saw Lily smile as she flew up and landed on top of one of Luis's horns. Panicking, I reached out and tried to snatch her from where she perched, but she quickly dodged out of the way, this time landing on Luis's head directly. I pressed my lips into a fine line and motioned for her to get back over to me. She simply looked up and away, refusing, so I whispered it this time, commanding her to come back. Lily sighed and flew back over to my shoulder. I could sense her frustration and confusion through our binding, and I pet her on the head softly to comfort her.

"Dinner is served!" Juli announced as she carried two plates of fish and vegetables over to the table.

Luis woke with a start just as Juli set a plate in front of him. He looked disoriented, looking at the plate for a few moments before he yawned a "thank you". Juli chuckled and set her plate down on the table in front of her seat before sitting down with us. We then spent the evening chatting and enjoying each other's company. About two hours had passed, and Juli was about to get up to clean the dishes when a thought occurred to me.

"Juli, do you run your shop in the fall and winter too? If so how do you keep it stocked with flowers?" I asked, genuinely curious.

"Oh, I don't keep it open during late fall and all of winter. Instead I take quests. I'm part of Brightbane too, see?" Juli gestured up to the wall in the kitchen across from us where there hung a small yellow banner with the guild crest on it.

I looked at her in surprise that she had never mentioned it before. "What type of adventurer are you?"

"I'm sorta a mage. Here, let me get my staff, I'll show you," she said as she went over to the closet and took out what looked to be a quarterstaff. She brought it over to the table, and handed it to me. It had some weight to it, that was certain, but it also had intricate runes carved up and down the length of the staff. "I combine magic with my physical attacks to pack an extra punch," she boasted.

"What element of magic? This has all of the elemental runes on it." I ran my fingers over the carved runes.

"Mostly I prefer water magic since it's my innate individual, but I know several spells in every element," she explained as I handed the staff back to her. She looked the staff over carefully as though inspecting a rare gem, and then nodded before moving to put it back in the closet.

"You know she's a better fighter than me. She's part of one of the best parties in Brightbane, the Raven Legion. They're really amazing to see in battle. I was lucky enough to get to train under them when I first started at the guild." Luis bragged for Juli, reaching across the table and playfully punching her on the shoulder as she sat down.

"Oh, can it, Rocky," she said with emphasis on the name, as though knowing it would annoy him.

He pouted his lower lip, crossed his eyes, and proceeded to repeat back what she had said in a mocking voice. Juli, not missing a beat, leaned over and grabbed his pouted lower lip between her fingers. Luis wilted and leaned towards her as she pulled hard on his lip.

"Ok, ok! Hint taken!" Luis begged, and Juli gave him a slight smile before releasing him.

"So, who's up for a game?" Juli clasped her hands together as she changed the subject and Luis rubbed his lip, defeated.

We then played a simple, luck-based game of rolling dice and moving our pieces along the board until we landed on certain traps after which we'd have to roll above a certain number to get out of them. It was fun, and Luis and Juli ended up getting very competitive in a light-hearted sort of way. At the end of our time with Juli, she made me promise that I would work on the knitted squares again now that I was home. Juli walked us out so that she could let down the forcefield for us, and waved to us as we left. Luis lit a torch to light our walk back home, but he did so hastily as though nervous about something. I decided to ignore it, figuring he must just be tired after a long day.

The next morning, I awoke to the sound of Luis rifling through his dresser drawers. "Damn, do I not own anything formal?" he muttered to himself. He then saw I was awake and chuckled nervously. "I guess I've been found out. Oh well, I needed to tell you at some point today anyway."

"Tell me what?" I asked, his anxiety sneaking into my mind as well.

"I've got a date! Only problem is, I don't seem to own any nice clothes and I've got to be formal. I mean, she didn't say I had to but-" Luis rambled and turned back to searching through the drawers.

My veins filled with sludge and my stomach boiled at the idea of him going on a date. It didn't matter with who, though it was more than likely Juli, all that mattered was that I had the sudden realization that I was losing him. There was no convincing him or making our relationship into "something more" like Margub

150

had encouraged. There was now only him, Juli, and their relationship. The cold steel of doubt sliced into my mind. *What if he doesn't want to watch over me anymore? What if he wants to live with Juli and I'll have to find other accommodations? What if, what if…* I thought of these doubts one after the other. But nothing trumped the painful reality of the situation. I wanted to be mad at Juli, to be furious and scream at her, but all I had in my heart for her was respect and fondness. I may not have been happy about this, but surely I could try to be happy *for* them or at least pretend to be.

I spent the first few hours of my day lingering around Luis, helping him with anything I could think to help with. But then the time came for him to leave, as he had to go get something to wear from the tailor in town and would then go straight to his date. I waved him off with a large fake smile that he was likely too anxious to see through, and walked back into the empty house alone. I contemplated working on my knitting, but I found that I had started crying. I needed a safe place now that Luis was away, and I only knew of one. I spent the rest of the day and that night curled up in the hall closet, clutching Lily, waiting, sobbing.

Chapter 17:

Good Friends and Good Ale

After an amazing date at the tavern and an even more amazing evening spent at Juli's house, I was over the moon as I returned home the next morning. I figured Ipris would still be asleep when I got back, so I snuck in, closing the door quietly behind me. I had stopped at the market to replenish our stock of groceries, and after getting everything put away, I made myself some eggs and toast for breakfast with some tea, and got cozy on the couch as I ate. About an hour had passed by the time I finished eating, and yet there was still no sign of Ipris. Getting a little worried, I went over to the bedroom and peeked inside. My stomach dropped in fear as I saw that she wasn't there. Trying not to panic, I quickly went out the front door and around back to see if she was in the garden, but she wasn't there either. I turned in a circle twice, at a loss for where she possibly could've gone, when a thought occurred to me. *No, it can't be,* I thought as I went back inside where I went over to the closet and slowly opened the door.

Inside the closet, just as I had guessed, was a sleeping Ipris holding Lily to her chest. She stirred a bit as the light hit her face and I bent down to gently shake her awake. I touched her shoulder, and her eyes snapped open as she woke with a start. Lily seemed to wake up as well, and before I could ask Ipris why she had hidden in the closet again, Lily flew up and started furiously pecking at my face and squawking. I fell backwards onto my butt and tried to shield my face from her. Ipris ordered Lily to stop, and after giving me a glare, Lily did so obediently.

"Yikes, what did I ever do to her?" I chuckled and rubbed my face.

I expected Ipris to laugh as well, or at least respond to what I had said. But instead, she completely changed the subject. "Did you already eat? Should I make you some breakfast?"

I looked at her with a furrowed brow. "What? Oh, no. I mean yes I did eat, and no you shouldn't make me some."

Ipris nodded and stood up, offering me a hand to help me. The three of us then went over to the living room, where Ipris started knitting, and I decided to nap on the couch to get some much needed rest since I hadn't gotten very much the night before. Before I fell asleep, I looked over to Ipris as she stared out the window, her eyes filled with melancholy. I didn't understand why she would be sad, but I didn't have the energy to ask her about it at that very moment as I fell right to sleep.

Four hours passed, and I awoke to the sound of a heavy knock at the door. I got up from the couch groggily and wandered over to the door. On the other side, were some familiar faces, my old adventuring party who had come to the door with a donkey-drawn wagon a little ways behind them. I threw my arms open wide to embrace each of the five as we all cheered at our meeting once again and I failed to remember Clark's warning. I had journeyed with this particular adventuring party two years before, and we had been very good friends. Though things didn't end overly amicably due to my dislike of their shoddy morals and greed, we had agreed to stay friends and I intended to honor that promise. They clearly intended to do so as well as they greeted me with wide smiles and hugged me back happily. Among the five were Groggut the berserker and Dwarf man, Penelope the rogue and Ekek woman, Ms. Grey the sorcerer and Vampire woman, Ryul the druid and Lauman (Life Fairy) man, and Vrang the bard and Werewolf man.

As soon as we had finished our greetings, I leaned against the door frame as I chuckled. "It's good to see you all again. So, what brings you to my neck of the woods?"

"Oh we've got a quest pretty near here and thought we'd ask if you wanted to come along. Word's been said to be an evil dragon that's made its way into the plains here and is causing havoc for some nearby farmers and shepherds," Groggut explained.

I tilted my head side to side a few times weighing the options. "I don't know, I mean that sounds pretty dangerous," I said hesitantly, thinking that bringing the kid along for this type of quest wouldn't be a good idea.

The group of them laughed thinking I was joking, but I stepped aside in the doorframe to show them Ipris. "Oh yeah, that's the girl Mika told us about! Don't worry, since it's a more dangerous quest she can stay behind. Surely, she'll be alright for a day and a half on her own?" insisted Vrang.

I scrunched my face, still unsure about it, but then Groggut chimed in again. "Well let's not make any decisions too hastily. We've brought a barrel of fine ale with us, and we intend it to go home empty!"

I chuckled, shaking my head. "Alright, alright. That sounds like a good enough arrangement to me. Come on in, and I'll make us all some lunch."

The five of them sauntered in and made themselves at home, some choosing a chair and others the couch. My living room hadn't been this filled with people in a long time, and I made my way into the kitchen to make us all some sandwiches while the party introduced themselves to Ipris. As I put them together, I overheard the group telling some stories to Ipris. I was a little concerned, though, as usually Ipris chimed in with a laugh or question when told a story, but as they talked to her, she remained

154

silent. I also overheard them asking about Lily, to which Ipris answered shortly and without detail. I carried the sandwiches over a few minutes later, each one wrapped in a hand towel, and handed them out amongst them. I then sat next to Groggut and Ms. Grey on the couch as I bit into my sandwich.

We all thoroughly enjoyed ourselves, eating and telling stories to our heart's content for several hours. After this, a pause came into our conversation, and I suggested that we all train together for a bit at my training grounds to get back in our rhythm of fighting together.

"Oh? So, you will be joining us on the quest, then?" Ms. Grey spoke up.

I looked to Ipris, still worried about her as she had been fairly withdrawn the entire time. "I suppose it's up to Ipris, here. Would you be ok on your own for a little while again?" I asked gently.

Ipris immediately nodded and insisted that she'd be fine if I wanted to go with them. My friends cheered as Ipris smiled resignedly, and though I was still concerned, I figured that we could talk once I got back from the quest. For now, we all decided to train together for a few more hours, drink and eat dinner, and then head out early the next morning. Ipris and Lily came with us to the training ground, as I didn't want to leave them alone right away. For the most part, we worked on our teamwork and combining attacks and abilities, but after we were in good enough sync, the group decided to help the kid with her training. While everyone had been working, she had been running around the track with Lily following behind her, but when they called her over and insisted on training with her, she got hard to work. She sparred with Groggut, Penelope, and me, and practiced her magic with Ms. Grey, Ryul, and Vrang while Lily watched patiently, occasionally squawking words of encouragement. All in all, she showed us that even though she had only a month's training, she was pretty well set to take care of herself, for low level quests at least.

After training, we headed back to the house, and my friends insisted on having a campfire cookout. I flew over to the nearest tree grove with Ryul to chop wood and gather kindling, as I didn't have any at home since I used magic items called fire plates to heat my stove, oven, and cauldron. We worked hard to gather the wood and kindling, and afterwards, Ryul used some magic to grow some seeds from the tree we had cut down into saplings. I also sent Penelope with some money to fly over to town and pick up a bunch of meat and bread, since although I had just gotten groceries that morning, there wasn't enough of any one thing for everyone. It took about an hour to prepare everything and get back to the house, but once we did, we all relaxed, ate, and drank in front of the campfire while Lily and Ipris stayed inside the house. At the end of the night, after many stories and much reminiscing, they set up in bedrolls in the living room, and I slept on the couch as usual.

The next morning, Ipris woke us up by cooking us all some breakfast of omelets and pickled shallots, which we quickly devoured, and then started packing up, getting ready to head out on the quest. I packed as many weapons and rations as I could fit, just in case, and went over and knelt in front of Ipris. She still looked pretty down, so I reached out a hand to her cheek.

"I'll be back before you know it. Ok? Take care of yourself and Lily, yeah?" I said and started to get up and turn away, but then turned back as a thought occurred to me. "And no hiding in the closet again. You can garden or knit or go into town and hang out with Juli for all I care. But no closet! Promise me!" I held up my pinky finger, which she silently wrapped her pinky finger around and smiled softly. I gave her cheek one last pinch and then I walked out the door with the rest of the group.

With the ale barrel drained from the night before, about four of us were able to ride in the back of the wagon, so we took turns walking and riding. An hour into our journey as we headed directly south, away from any sort of road or path, I thought to ask them something. "So how far away is this dragon?"

"'Bout six hours," Groggut responded grumpily, and I assumed that he was a little hungover from the night before.

From there, we traveled silently, and as we got closer, Penelope insisted on switching with Groggut so that he would be rested before the fight. They switched, and we started walking again, only about thirty minutes away from our destination. But I forgot one thing as I walked; Penelope was a rogue, and as she walked behind me, I never had a chance of hearing her unsheathe her blade. White-hot burning pain sprouted from my stomach as she rapidly wrapped her arms around me and slit open my stomach with a large gash of her dagger.

"Oh, would you look at that? Looks like I've slain the dragon all on my own!" she whispered triumphantly in my ear.

I grabbed at the pain, blood covering my hands as I fell to my knees. There was a ringing in my ears as I began to feel extremely light headed, so I didn't hear them get out of the wagon. But I realized that that's what had happened when Groggut held my head up by the throat. I struggled to focus my eyes on him, and I almost lost consciousness entirely, when he slapped me hard and I looked up at him, my vision a bit clearer.

"Why?" I managed to croak out.

Groggut smiled evilly. "Ever since you made the *selfish* decision to leave our group, we've been getting scraps for quests and money. And on top of that, we heard that you've been making more than your fair share. Taking jobs from Mika directly. And working for the URA?! Well that just isn't fair to little old us!"

I stared in horror. I had always known them to be greedy, but enough to kill a party member over it? I never would've thought them capable. I felt someone unhook my coin pouch from my bag and Vrag began boasting about how much of a payday this was for them. At this point, Groggut dropped me, and I slumped fully to the ground. As they walked away, a few of them spitting on me for good measure as they did so, all I could think of was Ipris and Juli. Once I could no longer hear their wagon, I pulled some bandages from my bag, and hastily began work on stuffing my organs back into place and covering over the wound with the gauze. It wasn't good work, but it didn't need to be. I forced myself to get up fully, yelling in pain a bit as I did, and then using the last of my energy, I began to make the excruciating flight back home. I didn't know if I would even make it that far, but I had to try.

Chapter 18:

Goodbye

As soon as Luis left for his quest, I decided to take the walk over to Tithridge, as I had had an idea to make an amazing dinner for when Luis returned. My throat closed at the thought that I had worried him by being so upset, and I was determined to make it up to him. Admittedly, there was also a small part of me that hoped beyond any sense or reason that I could win him over somehow. So, with this delusion in the back of my mind, I arrived in Tithridge. By this point, many of the shopkeepers knew my name, and treated me very kindly since I had always been by Luis's side. I stopped at many of the grocery stalls in the market, and proceeded to pick the highest quality ingredients I could find. It would likely cost me more than a few of my silver, but I wanted this meal to blow him out of the water so to speak. So I finished up my shopping about an hour later and was ready to head home when I accidentally bumped into someone.

I instantly bowed and apologized, worried that they would be upset with me, but instead I heard a kind voice. "Ipris? What are you doing here all by your lonesome, hun?" asked Juli who leaned down to look me in the eyes.

I straightened up and fought with both the urge to hug her and the urge to slap her. I decided on the former, and gave her a tight hug. "I'm getting some groceries for dinner tonight. I'm going to make Luis something to congratulate him." The lie slipped past my lips smoothly, and Juli had no reason to question it.

"Oh? What's the special occasion?" she directed us over to the side of the road as she asked so we wouldn't be blocking the flow of the crowd.

I sat down on a bench, carefully setting my groceries in my lap as Lily flew over to Juli's shoulder. "He went on a quest with some of his friends. He said it was too dangerous for me to go, though."

"Friends? What were their names? Maybe I know them," she said enthusiastically as she sat down next to me, giving Lily little pets with her finger.

"Groggut, Penelope, Ms. Grey, Ryul, and Vrang," I recited from memory.

Juli's expression soured. "Oh, I see."

"What is it?" I asked, tilting my head slightly to the side.

"Nothing, it's just, I never liked those guys. They had their priorities twisted and they were greedy as all hell. I was the one that convinced Luis to leave their group originally, actually."

"Will he be ok?" My voice cracked with concern.

Juli put an arm around my shoulders. "Of course! He's a big boy, he can take care of himself just fine. I just meant that I hope he doesn't get dragged into a bad quest because of them. But again, he'll be fine!" Juli insisted, and then stood up, offering me a hand. "You have some spare time? I can teach you a new knitting pattern!" She tilted her voice playfully.

I suddenly felt a cool wave of relief wash over me. I never should've had negative feelings toward Juli to begin with. Even if I felt bad imagining her and Luis together, both of them were such good people. I decided then and there to root for their relationship, no matter how bad the inky blackness in my heart got. I nodded in

160

affirmation of this and inadvertently agreed to go along with Juli. Not that her company wasn't welcomed now, but I had planned on getting back home soon to start preparing the meal. I followed along behind her anyway, though, and we headed over to her store. We spent the next hour chatting and knitting as Juli taught me a beautiful pattern that I decided would make up most of my squares from now on. After an hour had passed, though, I politely excused myself, and began to make my way home.

The two-hour walk passed peacefully, and I spent most of it whistling a tune back and forth with Lily. But, as we walked over the hill, Lily squawked and darted off towards the house. At first, I didn't see why, but then my stomach dropped as I saw Luis lying in a heap. I dropped my bags, no longer caring if the ingredients got damaged or not and sprinted over to him. My mind swirled, hoping beyond hope that he was just tired from journeying back from the quest. But as I reached him, I saw the bloody bandages wrapped around his stomach. For a moment, I froze. This couldn't be happening, surely I must've been dreaming. But it was real as Luis groaned weakly and looked up at me from the ground. I knelt next to him and took one of his hands in mine.

I rubbed his hand between my hands over and over again in a panic. "Hey, you're ok, right? You're going to be ok!" My voice began to crack and falter as tears stung at my eyes. Luis looked at me helplessly, and I quickly stood as I let go of his hand. "I'll get a doctor! You stay right here!" I declared and turned to begin to run off, but Luis grabbed the hem of my dress to stop me.

"No, Ipris there's no time. Listen to me, ok?" Luis said sternly, in a voice he had never used with me before. I knelt back down beside him and nodded. He reached out and pressed his hand to my cheek softly, his hand still wet with the cruel touch of blood. He smiled up at me weakly, and I put both of my hands over his hand as tears spilled from my eyes. "You remember what I always said, yeah? You're freaking fantastic, and you *never* forget

161

that. Ok?" he croaked out, and it dawned on me, he was saying goodbye. At this realization I began fully sobbing as I held tightly to his hand and nodded. "Hey, don't cry. You're gonna be just fine, ya know? Just fine…" he started to trail off as he struggled to keep his eyes open.

"Luis! Hey, *you're* going to be fine. We can both be fine right? Please tell me I'm right, Luis!" I begged, gripping even tighter onto his hand.

He opened his eyes again and spoke to me with labored breaths, "Ipris, I-" he started, but dropped off as his eyes lost their light and his hand fell limply from my cheek.

"No! No, no, no! Don't you leave me! Luis!" The words tore from my throat in a scream as I began to rock back and forth and clutched my hands to my chest. I sobbed for a few minutes before managing to croak out, "You were supposed to be my forever. I love---" I cut myself off with my own shaking. "I loved you…" I whispered, setting my forehead on his ever-cooling body. I sat there crying like that for hours, and only got pulled out of it when I heard footsteps running up behind me. I turned to look, and saw that Lily had led Juli to us…to me. I flinched, expecting her to scream at me, blame me, but she ran up and hit her knees as she wrapped me in a hug.

"Hey, it's ok. It's ok, hun. You're gonna---" she faltered in her trying to console me as she broke down into tears as well.

We sat there, crying in each other's arms until Juli eventually leaned back from me and wiped my cheeks with one of her hands. "We're gonna be just fine, hun. We're gonna get through this." She squeezed me tightly one last time before standing.

I stood as well with her help, and we began discussing what to do. It felt surreal, talking about how to bury the only person I'd ever loved, but it had to be done. We spent the next few hours until sunset burying him next to his garden. I had cried so much that during this entire process, I dug robotically, not thinking about anything, just digging. Juli and I took off his pack and armor and carefully lowered him into the hole. When it was done, and Juli started filling in the grave, I decided to search his belongings for some kind of will or journal or note. I didn't find one, but I also couldn't find his coin pouch, and my veins began to burn as my heart swirled with fire. I realized exactly what had happened, exactly who had done this. They had killed him for his money, for their *greed*. The heat rose through me, and I stood, dropping the pack limply.

"Woah, uh, you're on fire, hun!" Juli said in a panic and I looked at my hands, expecting to see flames. There weren't any, however, and I gave her a confused look, to which she merely pointed above my head. I reached up to my wick, and sure enough, my wick had lit on fire. Though like my spells, it wasn't melting me at all.

I lowered my hands and clenched them into fists as I changed the subject. "Juli, they took his money. They *killed* him and stole from him...I'm going to *slaughter* them," I said in a low voice, malice lining my words.

Juli set down her shovel and walked over to me. It looked like she had several things she wanted to say and couldn't pick which one to start with. But then she looked me in the eyes, put her hands on my shoulders and said, "Is that what he would want?"

I looked down and away from her, I wanted to tell her that I didn't care if it's what he wanted because it's what they deserve. I wanted to storm off and grab my spear and shield to kill them all as soon as possible. But her words stung, because in the back of my head I could hear him saying the line from the book we had read together. And though they weren't his words, they held the same meaning as if he had said them. "He wouldn't want me to become

163

the monster…" I fought back tears, but Juli pulled me into a hug, and I let them spill down my face once more.

I steeled myself again after a moment and Juli leaned back from our hug to look me in the eyes once more. "Ok, so we don't *murder* them, but that doesn't mean we can't try to make this right. I'm going to go to Cadmar and report this to the guild, get those bastards locked away forever. Do you want to come with me?"

* * *

At first, we went to Swindon to bring Luis's dad and sister news of his death. They were both heartbroken, but his sister seemed to get the brunt of it all as she became very ill shortly after hearing the news. We offered to stay to care for her, when to our surprise, Luis's father offered to do so instead, insisting that it was what Luis would want. From there, Juli and I went to Cadmar together, and though we had a few hiccups like Lily's existence and the guards not liking her, we were able to report Luis's murder to the guild and the guards. It wasn't hard to find the party that killed him, nor was it difficult to prove they had been the ones to kill him as they had been in Cadmar recklessly spending the money they got off of Luis. That coupled with a few drunken confessions, and they were locked up for good, sentenced to life in prison and kicked out of the guild. Not wanting to go back to Tithridge just yet, and the URA still requiring someone to watch over me, I traveled with Juli for about a year after that, training under her party, the Raven Legion. I wasn't as good as them by the end of it all, but I was good enough to keep up and support them where they needed me to.

When Juli and I parted ways in Cadmar, it was because I had decided to find a new place for myself. Juli argued that I always had a place with her, but as good of a friend as she was, she also reminded me of sour memories. I didn't tell her this, though, and simply insisted I wanted to focus on studying for a little while.

From there, I went to the place that had promised me a sanctuary in any time of need; I went to the temple of Qilios and studied under Margub. I learned many practices while I was there, both religious and not, until it came time for Margub to pass on as well. Before he parted from this world, he insisted on making me a priestess. It was hard for me to lose a mentor of so many years, and though I still wasn't very religious after all that time, I dutifully took up the mantle. I gained much knowledge and a bit of magic as a priestess of Qilios, but most importantly, I gained the ability to help others the way I had been helped.

I helped many people as a priestess of Qilios, and in turn it helped me to recognize my own feelings, not just those of others. Many more years passed, and as I remained ageless, the people around me aged and passed on in what felt like rapid succession. I watched Mika and even Juli pass before I decided to reconnect with my siblings, leave Cadmar, and travel with them as a Cleric, a priestess adventurer. The first place I visited was Swindon, there were a few people there whose faces I recognized, but they were scarred by age. I then made my way to Tithridge where it was much the same as Swindon. The final place I visited before going on the quests that would change my life forever was Luis's grave.

I knelt down in front of the headstone at the house that had been largely torn down over the years of being vacant and prayed. "I hope you are well in whatever afterlife you ended up at, reincarnation or not, so long as you are happy. Forgive me for not shedding any tears, but the many years since I lost you have been both wonderful and cruel, but also very full of tears…I never loved another, you know. Not the way I loved you. No one could live up to the great Luis Rockwell! I know Juli found another and had children, but I hope you two found each other after everything, if not for love, then for friendship. You two still deserve each other, even now…especially now. I won't be back to visit for quite some time. I'll be travelling all across Aethos, perhaps even the world!

Helping others, going on adventures…Right, well I won't bother your rest any longer. Goodbye, Luis Rockwell."

———————

The End